a Suitcase Tale

Marcia

Linda Bishop Foley

InspiringVoices®
A Service of **Guideposts**

Inspiring Voices books may be ordered through booksellers or by contacting:

Inspiring Voices
1663 Liberty Drive
Bloomington, IN 47403
www.inspiringvoices.com
1-(866) 697-5313

Because of the dynamic nature of the Internet, any web addresses or links contained in this book may have changed since publication and may no longer be valid. The views expressed in this work are solely those of the author and do not necessarily reflect the views of the publisher, and the publisher hereby disclaims any responsibility for them.

Any people depicted in stock imagery provided by Thinkstock are models, and such images are being used for illustrative purposes only.
Certain stock imagery © Thinkstock.

ISBN: 978-1-4624-0391-2 (sc)
ISBN: 978-1-4624-0392-9 (e)

Library of Congress Control Number: 2012920150

Printed in the United States of America

Inspiring Voices rev. date: 11/21/2012

This book is dedicated to my wonderful friends who encouraged me to write, made helpful corrections, typed, proof read, and edited. I couldn't have done it without them.

Chapter *One*

Marcia studied the contents of a small beige Samsonite which lay open on her mother's bed. It was half full. Perhaps she had missed something. She returned to the armoire. The heavy odor of stale cigarette smoke and strong perfume assailed her nose. How she hated sharing this, the only closet space in the apartment, with her mother, Julia, and youngest sister, Collette. Everyone's clothes reeked, and if Collette forgot to close the armoire's doors, her cat, Pepper, climbed in and deposited hair on the bottoms of their skirts and in all their shoes. Marcia had retrieved every piece of her clothing. She sighed as she shut the door.

Marcia walked through the kitchen. Her mother and Minnie, her mother's best friend, were seated at the table having coffee and smoking cigarettes. Marcia entered the enclosed back porch and collected a long plastic bag which was tightly knotted at the bottom and had a metal hanger protruding from a tiny opening in the top. She had chosen the highest nail on the porch wall, well out of the cat's reach, and hopefully away from the cigarette smoke, on which to hang her bundle. The bag contained her "essential black dress."

Mother had accompanied her to one of the two exclusive dress shops in town and, to Marcia's extreme mortification, loudly announced to all present the reason for their errand. Marcia retreated to the dressing room

1

with the first outfit they found. She could hear her mother's incessant chatter as she followed the clerk around the shop and felt sorry for the woman. They soon found a simple wool dress and matching three-quarter sleeve jacket. The sales lady had emphasized that this dress could be accessorized in so many ways, was so very stylish, and would be perfect for any function Marcia might attend. The dress did fit well and looked elegant. Her mother happily agreed with the clerk as to the merits of the ensemble, and paid an enormous sum so that Marcia could have it. The cost bothered Marcia, but her mother was insistent. She would add it to her charge account. Marcia knew it would be a long time before the account was paid in full.

Now she hesitated, bag across her arm, listening to the falsetto tones in her mother's voice as she repeated, for at least the hundredth time, how proud she was that her oldest daughter had chosen nursing. This was always followed by, "I always wanted to be a nurse. Should have gone right after high school. What was I thinking ?" There would be a brief pause, then, "Well, Marcia's going to do it."

Marcia passed through the kitchen.

"Are you all packed?"

"Just need to put this in the suitcase and I'll be ready."

"The cab's here," Collette hollered from the front porch. The screen slammed behind her as she ran into the room.

"Couldn't you just come and get me? You always yell from the porch."

Collette's cheeks reddened.

"Come give me a kiss. I love you." The sisters gave each other a long hug. Marcia released Collette and pulled her suitcase off the bed.

The cabby was leaning on the horn.

"Bye, Mom. Thanks for everything." Marcia gave her mother a quick hug and headed for the cab; her mother, Minnie, and Collette on her heels. Her mother was wringing her hands and making the funny moans and noises she always made when she was excited. Marcia found this very annoying and wished they all had stayed in the house, especially after Collette stepped on the back of her shoe and caused her to trip.

"This it?" asked the driver as she handed him the suitcase and a small matching cosmetic case, a gift she had received from her father when she graduated from high school.

Marcia nodded.

"Where to?"

"The train depot."

Marcia glanced out the window as the cab turned the corner. Her mother was waving frantically with one hand and wiping away tears with the other. Collette had found Pepper and had buried her face in her fur.

"Where you headed?"

"I'm going to St. Joseph's in Denver. I'm starting nurse's training."

"Well, I think that's great," the driver replied. He then launched into a story about his Uncle Ed's gallbladder surgery. He thought the nurses were great, but didn't care much for the doctor.

Marcia was grateful the ride was short. She was sure the driver had a number of tales he would be all too happy to relate.

She settled herself on the train. The compartment was only half-full so she had the seat to herself. She felt a churning in her stomach. Four hundred and thirty-six dollars and fifty-six cents was the total contents of her purse. What if she didn't have enough money to cover the first year's expenses? How could she have considered going to Denver with such a small amount?

Mother was not good at giving advice.

"What in the world prompted me to follow her advice this time? I must have been out of my mind. Oh well, it's done. I'll just have to hope for the best.", Marcia contemplated ruefully.

She had told Julia about her visit to the O'Shea's. Mrs. O'Shea was a graduate of St. Joseph's and volunteered to give Marcia and her friend, Janet, one of the required recommendations needed to enter training. Marcia gladly accepted the assistance. Janet declined as she was gong to the University of Wyoming.

Marcia received all the required recommendations and completed the paperwork necessary to apply. In early spring, a letter inviting her to take the entrance exam arrived. Julia was beside herself with excited anticipation.

Marcia took her exam in late April. It had not seemed particularly hard, but she was quite relieved when a thick manila envelope arrived a month later. She had been accepted. All of the necessary paperwork was enclosed, including a sheet detailing expenses for the three years. Marcia's relief was replaced by a surge of panic.

She had understood that the cost for the three years of training, room, board, books, and tuition was supposed to be six hundred dollars. That was the amount quoted when she had inquired last year. The enclosed paperwork indicated the cost was now one thousand dollars.

The explanation for the increase of four hundred dollars was no comfort. She would only have a bit over four hundred dollars saved by the end of the summer!

Marcia was waiting in the kitchen when Julia returned from work. "I'm not going to be able to go to St. Joe's."

"Why?" her mother's voice trembled.

"The costs have risen to a thousand dollars. Where will I ever get the extra money?"

Julia settled on a kitchen chair and lit a cigarette.

"My feet hurt." She removed her white oxfords and began to massage her right foot. She gave a deep sigh of contentment as she rubbed.

"MOM! What about school?"

"You can still go."

"How do you figure that?" Marcia replied irritably. She grabbed the expense sheet and thrust it at her mother.

Julia glanced at the paper.

"You don't have to pay for all three years at once. Just pay for the first year."

"Then what?"

"Something will come up. Maybe they'll have some jobs for students, and I'll help."

Judging from the fifteen dollars her mother had put away for her education, Marcia knew she would not be a reliable source of financial help. Julia could barely support the three of them on her income, even when tips were good.

"Mom, I won't have enough money."

"Even if you have to come home after a year, you'll have that much education. No one will be able to take that away from you. If you have to leave, you can work at the hospital as an aide until you've saved enough to start again."

At the time it sounded workable. With her stomach still churning, Marcia rethought the dollar she had paid for the cab fare to the depot. Perhaps she should have taken her father and step-mother's offer. She couldn't help the rising unpleasant feelings as she recalled the offer and the scene that accompanied it.

She had been invited to dinner at their home, which was located in a new housing division on the north side of town. After a simple dinner, they moved to the comfortable living room. Dad and Velma were seated on the divan. Marcia sat in a plush chair that faced them.

"So you've decided on nursing? You don't want to go to Casper Junior College?" her father asked.

"With your grades you could be a teacher or a secretary," Velma added.

"I think I'll try nursing."

"We've been thinking too," Louis said, "I know that you're considering St. Joseph's. It's Catholic, isn't it?"

Marcia knew her father had no doubts about the school's affiliation.

"Yes it is."

"Well, Velma and I wondered if you'd considered St. Luke's? It's in Denver too."

"No Dad, I haven't. St. Luke's is Episcopalian."

"You'd get a very good education at St. Luke's." Velma's voice had an guarded edge to it.

"I'm sure I would, but I'm Catholic and I want to learn Catholic medical ethics. I won't be doing that if I train at St. Luke's," Marcia explained.

"We want you to know that if you choose St. Luke's, Velma and I would pay for every bit of your training. You still have time to apply."

Marcia sat in stunned silence. Her mother didn't always receive the paltry court-ordered support, yet now they were offering to pay for her entire education. She would not have to do without or worry about costs!

It was a fleeting temptation.

"Dad, I feel it's important that I go to St. Joe's."

"Well, young lady," Velma hotly interjected, "if you make that choice you need to understand that we won't pay one penny, not one, toward your education. Do I make myself clear?"

"Yes, quite clear."

Velma continued, "Why you want to be associated with a religion that considers you and your sisters bastards, I'll never understand!"

Marcia's face flushed.

"The Church doesn't consider me or my sisters illegitimate."

"I'm sure you're aware that your parents were never married in the Catholic Church!"

"That doesn't mean we're illegitimate. They had a civil ceremony. I think I'd better be going. Thank you for dinner." Marcia rose from her chair.

Her father rose also. "I'll drive you home."

Velma remained seated, her gaze directed out the picture window. They made the drive home in a depressing silence. When he pulled up to the curb, Louis asked if she would reconsider her decision.

"Dad, I'm going to St. Joe's."

"I'm very disappointed in you," he said quietly. "I thought you would be more sensible."

Marcia leaned over to kiss his cheek. He sat stiffly, looking straight ahead with both hands gripping the steering wheel.

She exited the car and hurried up the steps without looking back. Her heart was heavy and her eyes smarted. She paused on the porch and took several deep breaths. When she entered the apartment her face was composed.

She found her mother and Collette at the kitchen table eating ice cream. She could tell that her mother was anxious to hear the details of her visit, but Marcia was definitely not interested in sharing. She spoke quickly.

"We had dinner and discussed my schooling. Dad and Velma want me to go to St. Luke's. I told them I'm going to St. Joe's. Any ice cream left?"

Julia knew from her daughter's tone that any questions were useless, so she nodded and pointed to the refrigerator.

"There's a little peach left in the carton."

Marcia dug in the drawer until she found a spoon and emptied the scant contents into a bowl. She joined her mother and sister at the table.

"Well, I have some news for you," Julia chirped. "Lee Ann just told me she is PG again. I don't know what she's thinking...seventeen and a year of school to finish."

Marcia gave an exasperated sigh.

"What were YOU thinking? You let her date way too early and get married at fifteen. Babies generally come with marriage."

"It wasn't my fault," Julia whined, "they eloped."

"I told you to get it annulled. She was still living under your roof for heaven's sake!" Marcia's voice was sharp.

"You don't understand young love, or the agony of being torn apart." Julia half whispered.

"And what did your mother think when her barely sixteen-year-old daughter eloped ? She annulled it in a heartbeat and stuck you out on the ranch."

Julia looked like a hurt bewildered child and said wistfully, " I should have stayed married to Ed."

Marcia's voice softened.

"Mom, I don't know that you were any more prepared for marriage then than when you married Dad. I'm well aware that teenagers can fall in 'love'. Given, it can be a powerful experience, but time and distance, seem to make many young women look back and realize Mr. Wonderful wasn't all that great. Besides, there's got to be more to love than strong feelings. There just has to be."

The words, however true, were easy for Marcia to formulate but difficult for her to live by. Her own feelings often sabotaged her decisions concerning her relationships with the opposite sex.

Collette interrupted, "Is Lee Ann going to have another baby?"

"Hush dear, young ladies don't talk about those things." stated Julia.

"What things?"

"Just never you mind."

"What things are you talking about?"

"I'll tell you when you're older," Julia replied.

No you won't, Marcia thought. *Anything remotely concerning dating, men, or sex will never be discussed in this house.*

Marcia wished she'd seen more of Lee Ann this summer. Lee Ann had delivered her second son in July and Marcia had worked full time at the bakery. Their visits were strained when Marcia did come. Lee Ann stubbornly refused all offers of help. Marcia watched her struggle to nurse the squalling infant and manage her inquisitive toddler. She could hear the frustration in her sister's voice as she scolded the small boy peering from behind the couch.

"Why don't you let me take one of them for awhile?"

"I can manage."

"Well, I can give you a breather."

"I said I can manage."

The tiny house in north Casper, adjacent to Lee Ann's in-laws, was stifling. Marcia wondered what Lee Ann was trying to prove. Everything about her seemed to be changing. Her language could be harsh and the increasing frequency of profanity was appalling. She was developing a hard edge in her interactions with others. *Lee Ann wouldn't have married if I'd been home*, Marcia thought guiltily. *I should have been there.*

The train jolted to a stop. Several people entered the car. With the conductor's "All Aboard", they were on their way. The swaying of the train was soothing, almost like being rocked. Marcia took a deep breath and closed her eyes. She needed to make herself relax.

Chapter *Two*

"Are you coming Lee Ann," Marcia hissed through the basement window. "If you don't hurry Dad is going to ask us to watch Tagalong." Ten- and-a-half year old Marcia lay on the sparse grass next to the open window. She peered down at her sister who was hurriedly buckling her sandals.

"Come out the back door. Our bikes are by the garage."

Lee Ann raced up the stairs and slammed the screen as she ran into the yard.

"You idiot ! Collette will hear us!"

Marcia was right. As they mounted their bikes, Collette appeared on the front porch.

"Can I come too?"

"You'll have to ask Dad," Marcia called over her shoulder as she and Lee Ann scrambled through the gate. Collette ran back into the house calling for their father.

Quickly Marcia and Lee Ann disappeared down the alley, dust and pebbles flying in their wake. They stopped at several houses, but all their friends were gone, or if they were home, were doing chores and couldn't leave. They decided to find shade under the tree on the slope behind Mr. Posver's abandoned house.

"Collette won't see us here. Besides, she's not allowed to cross the street," Marcia said smugly.

"Don't you think it's kinda mean that we always ditch her?" Lee Ann asked timidly.

"Do you want her tagging along?"

"No, but I hate to see her cry."

"Well, you can go home and play with her if you like," said Marcia scornfully. "I get tired of pulling her in that damn wagon."

"She probably gets tired of it too. That's why she likes to play with us," Lee Ann explained patiently.

"Well I get mighty tired of you both!"

For a moment Lee Ann's bottom lip quivered and she blinked her eyes to hold back the gathering moisture.

"Oh good Lord, what are you crying about? I didn't say I hated you, I just get tired too. Aren't you glad to be out of the house? There's another fight coming."

"How do you know?"

"I heard Dad swearing about some damn thing and Mom had that look on her face."

While Lee Ann considered that information, Marcia jumped to her feet.

"Hey, look what I see!"

Three partially buried coke bottles lay baking in the hot afternoon sun next to a clump of garbage cans. Marcia wondered why anyone would be so stupid as to discard pop bottles. They were worth three cents apiece at Murray's Market. The smelly cans yielded another three bottles. The girls were elated.

"We can get a ton of candy. We can even bring some home for Collette. How's that ?" Lee Ann was pleased. Marcia handed her two of the bottles.

"Don't you dare drop these, or I swear, you won't get a thing."

Holding the bottles with one hand and steering with the other, the girls peddled to Murray's. A few minutes later they returned to the slope and opened a small brown bag. Marcia poured the contents into her lap. It yielded a feast of root beer barrels, Bit O Honeys, squares of chewy nougat, several orange slices, and a few lemon drops. They portioned out the candy evenly and set aside two pieces for Collette. They chewed in blissful silence. Lee Ann was unaware that a nickel from the refund remained in her sister's pocket.

The girls stretched out on the grass being careful to keep their skirts tucked under their legs. An observer would not have guessed them to be sisters. Marcia was very slender. Her short auburn hair curled around an oval face and softened the prominent nose and chin she had inherited from their father. Her dark brown eyes had a frank gaze which she used when she felt that she was not being observed; otherwise, she had a habit of keeping her eyes down and looking through partially open lids. It was a self defense strategy she had learned years earlier when life had been so hard. She had an olive complexion, high cheek bones crowned with a peachy flush, and a full bottom lip under a thinner top one. Her long legs were well shaped and already her breasts formed small mounds under her blouse. Her height and general manner made her seem much older than she was.

Nine year-old Lee Ann was average in height and had the soft roundness of childhood. She had thick, straight, chestnut hair and large brown eyes with long curly lashes. Her square pleasant face had a look of innocence. She had a well formed nose and chin and full lips. She too had high cheek bones, but possessed a beautifully creamy complexion. Although she tended toward shyness and Marcia usually dictated their activities, Lee Ann had a very strong, rarely seen stubborn streak.

Lee Ann pointed to several small clouds that scuttled across the bright blue Wyoming sky, "I think that one looks like a bird."

"Maybe."

They watched the clouds until they tired of their lazy transformations.

"Can we go look for birds?" asked Lee Ann hopefully, "We haven't been for days."

"Okay. Why don't we stop at home first. We can bring Collette with us."

Lee Ann smiled brightly at Marcia's suggestion.

The house was situated directly across the street from the oil and water tanks which serviced the soon-to-be retired steam engines. These structures stood sentry-like on tall stilt legs between the barren tracks and were the nesting place for pigeons and other small birds. The young who had the unfortunate experience of losing a place in the nest landed in the puddles which formed below the leaky tanks. Those that landed in oil usually did not survive, but the girls were undeterred by the probable outcome. They would scoop up any survivors of the precipitous drop and deposit them in a chicken wire and apple crate cage which sat in a corner of the front porch. Louis had made the cage for these occasions and had taught the girls to gently bathe the squawking chicks.

The birds underneath the water tanks fared better and some actually reached adulthood. It was always a tearful struggle for Lee Ann to open the cage door and allow the birds to return to the wild. Still, searching for birds remained one of their favorite pastimes.

As they parked their bikes behind the garage, Marcia gave an order, "Stay put behind the garage until I tell you to come."

"Why?"

"Just do as I say," Marcia replied firmly. She hunched down and took a position below the kitchen windows. She listened intently for a moment, stood up, and motioned to Lee Ann. They entered the house through the back door.

"Watch your step," Marcia sighed with exasperation.

A trickle of water flowed down the steps connecting the kitchen landing to the back door landing.

"You go ahead," Marcia said as she handed Lee Ann the brown bag. Lee Ann opened the door while Marcia knelt down on the top step and began to carefully move the overflowing basin under the icebox.

"Where did you get money for candy?" father's voice boomed. Lee Ann started to stammer.

Marcia called through the open door, "We found a few bottles and traded them in. We bought a treat for Collette. Thought she might like that. You don't mind, right Dad?"

His voice softened, "I'm glad you girls thought of your sister. She can have her treat after supper. Why aren't you coming in?"

"I've got to empty the drip pan," while under her breath Marcia muttered, "We wouldn't have this stupid mess if we had a refrigerator like everybody else."

Marcia gave the heavy pan a tug, sloshing more water on the floor. She was careful to keep her cursing in low tones. She pushed open the screen with her shoulder and flung the water into the backyard. A cat yowled.

"Oh, sorry Boots."

Once she had mopped the stairs and hung the rags on the clothesline to dry, she entered the kitchen.

"Is mom at work?"

"Yes, she is."

"Do you need help with anything?"

"No, I'll fix supper tonight. You'll be taking care of the girls the next two nights. I have union meetings and your mom works. You'll need to be in the house before your mother leaves at two."

Marcia knew that meant she wouldn't be seeing her best friend, Sally, for awhile.

"What are we having?"

"I thought liver would taste good. We haven't had any for some time," her father replied as he took a cast iron skillet from the pantry.

Marcia grimaced. Her father always bought the end chunks piled in the back of the meat tray and not the thin slices in the front of the case. She watched him coat the slimy chunks with flour. He poured stored bacon grease from a tin can perched on the metal shelf above the stove into the skillet. He struck a match and turned the closest knob. While he waited for the grease to heat, he checked a pan at the back of the stove.

"Are we having mashed potatoes?"

"Yes, and green beans. Get a can from the pantry, then you girls can set the table."

Beans and mashed potatoes, thought Marcia as they set the table. *At least grace won't be wasted.*

13

"Can we go look for birds?" asked Lee Ann.

"You girls need to stay here. Supper is almost ready."

"Dad, the table's all set and we'll just be across the street. Holler out the door. We'll come right back. We'll take Collette with us."

Collette clapped her hands and did a little dance.

"Pleeeze," she begged.

"Well, make sure you come when you're called," Louis turned back to the stove.

"And watch for cars!"

A few seconds of silence ensued as they headed to the door.

"And take Collette by the hand."

"Yes Dad," Marcia and Lee Ann answered. They were out the door before he could give more directions.

They had just enough time to search under all the tanks when they heard their father calling. They had no rescues that evening.

Dinner was predictable. Marcia and Lee Ann vied for the smallest piece of meat. The liver had arrived at the table with its usual presentation, a mound of black chunks piled on a plate. They reminded Marcia of lumps of coal. The chunks, when cut, yielded centers of bright pink paste with a most obnoxious smell and unappetizing taste. Marcia often wished they were burned all the way through. The girls wolfed down the potatoes and green beans. They cut the meat into tiny pieces. Then they would stare at the lacerated remnants which were fast becoming cold and had a shiny coat of congealed grease around the edges. They could usually manage to wash a few bites of black crust down with several gulps of milk. After what seemed like an eternity, they would be excused from the table.

"Are you sure you girls are full?"

They nodded vigorously.

"I guess I'll have to finish this by myself," Louis almost sounded apologetic as he scraped the scraps onto his plate.

Chapter *Three*

The train was slowing. Marcia jerked to wakefulness. She was surprised that she had dozed off. She didn't feel tired. Were they already in Cheyenne? The large crowd of new boarders was looking for seats. Marcia scooted toward the window. A nicely dressed older woman took the space. She inquired if Denver was Marcia's final destination. This was the start of a very pleasant conversation which lasted until their arrival at the Denver station. As they rose to leave, the older lady asked Marcia if she needed to arrive at the school at any particular time.

"No, I just have to check in this afternoon."

"Would you like to join me for lunch?"

Marcia realized that she was hungry, but she was acutely aware of her finances.

"Oh, that is so nice of you to ask, but I probably shouldn't," Marcia responded.

"I don't like eating alone. It would be my treat."

"Ohhh....I guess I could."

"I know just the place. We'll eat at Furr's. It's cafeteria style and they have a nice selection."

They stored the luggage in lockers at the depot and walked the few blocks to the restaurant. Marcia was impressed at the variety of choices and considered the arrangements beautiful. She was very grateful for the lunch. They lingered for a short time after dessert for more conversation and then went to retrieve their luggage. Marcia again thanked her companion and they exchanged goodbyes as they walked to separate cabs. She would not remember her name, but she would always remember the kindness of a stranger.

Marcia enjoyed the ride from the depot. St. Joseph's was surrounded by neighborhoods of large older houses and rows of brick brownstones. The school of nursing occupied a beautiful four story brown and tan art deco building. The first floor had elaborate woodwork and shiny marble floors. The parlors and library were separated by ornate French doors. It seemed like a palace. The hospital across the street was newer and the building wasn't nearly as interesting to Marcia.

The freshmen occupied the second floor. The elevator was off limits to them. It was reserved for the upper classmen who lived on the third and fourth floors. An exception was made for incoming students on arrival day. Marcia was instructed to take her luggage to her room and return to the office to complete registration and get her schedule. The textbooks were to be found in the library. Her heart pounded. If she could just get through the line. She felt like her hands were shaking. Hopefully no one would notice.

Marcia gave her name at the front desk and was directed toward the freshman section. She carefully selected her books, choosing from the used stack whenever she could. New workbooks were required and she needed notebooks for each class. Why did everything seem so expensive? Suddenly, Marcia found herself at the register. She carefully unloaded her arms and held her breath.

"You owe $427.38 Miss Gardinier."

A wave of relief swept over Marcia. She had enough money, even after the two cab fares. She paid her fees, scooped up her books and headed toward the exit. So what if she had only $3.69 left? She would find a way to make it. She was almost through the door when she noticed the sign.

OFFICE HELP WANTED
ANSWER PHONES AND GREET CALLERS
Sunday afternoons 1-4

See Sister Margaret Mary

Marcia wheeled around and returned to the cashier.

"Excuse me."

"Yes?" the woman frowned. Marcia had interrupted a transaction.

"Who's Sister Margaret Mary?"

"She's over there. The tall one."

Sister was tall, young, and quite pretty. She had a wide welcoming smile.

"Sister Margaret Mary?"

"Yes my dear."

"I'd like to apply for the job; the one on Sunday afternoons."

"Those books are heavy. Why don't you take them to your room and come to my office when you're done. It's right across the hall."

Marcia flew up the stairs. She was relieved and thankful. *If I get this job, I can make it. Three hours a week should be more than enough for any essentials I'll need. I should be able to save for some new clothes too.*

Sister explained all the requirements when Marcia met her in the office. Marcia would have to give up every Sunday afternoon.

"Many students have social activities then. Saturdays and Sundays are your only free time. Are you sure you would be willing to do that?"

Marcia assured Sister that she was definitely willing, so Sister gave her the job. She would receive a dollar per hour and would be paid weekly. She would start this coming Sunday. Marcia was elated and thanked her enthusiastically. Her remaining money would certainly last 'til payday.

Marcia started towards her room intent on looking through her books especially Anatomy and Physiology. She slowed half-way down the hall. A loud voice and equally loud music were coming from her room. Her newly arrived roommate was the source of the ruckus. When she saw Marcia, she clapped her soundly on the back. Jane was a tiny young woman. She was dressed in a well tailored brown suit. Her three inch heels seemed to add little to her height. Several pieces of gold jewelry accented her outfit and gold rings sparkled on her well manicured fingers. She had a cigarette dangling from her bottom lip which moved convulsively as she talked and gestured.

"How in the hell are you? I'm Jane Laussen. Guess you're my roomy. I'll get my trunk off your bed in a minute. My folks are taking it home."

Jane heaved a pile of clothes from Marcia's desk to her own bed which was hidden under a mountain of clothes and shoes.

"Mom and Dad, this is..."

"I'm Marcia Gardinier." Marcia moved across the room and extended her hand.

"Sister said Jane had a roommate from Wyoming," said Mr. Laussen as he shook hands.

"Yes, I'm from Casper."

"Oh, the big city. We're from Rawlins," he said smiling.

"Casper's really growing. How large is it now?" asked Mrs. Laussen.

"I heard it's approaching forty thousand. Don't think we'll beat Cheyenne though."

The Laussens were ready to leave. They seemed like nice people, very quiet. Marcia felt sorry for them. Jane was very loud, her speech peppered with profanity, and she was a chain smoker, all the things Marcia found distasteful. Jane gave the impression that the room was totally hers and that Marcia was a necessary intruder. Marcia immediately realized that they would not be friends and hoped she would be able to change roommates soon. She would quickly discover that her suspicions regarding Jane's housekeeping skills were correct; Jane's side of the room would be a constant disaster. She was relieved when the housemother came to get them for a welcoming cook-out in the rear yard.

A soft breeze cooled the warm night and the yard crowded with all three classes. Marcia was delighted to meet the other students and stayed as far away from Jane as she could. She found Judy, another Wyoming girl, and spent most of the evening with her.

Chapter *Four*

Jane was finally asleep. She made a little hum when she exhaled. Marcia's bed was by the window nearest the hospital. She had opened it halfway for the fresh air. She was here at nurses' training. She had made it thus far and was excited by the prospects before her. She had felt that same excitement about Midwest Street too. She remembered the first day she and Lee Ann had seen the house. They ran up and down the basement stairs and played tag on the main floor. They could circle through the entire first floor by going from the living room to the kitchen, then through the bathroom and into their parent's bedroom which led back to the living room. A heavy maroon curtain hanging from a thick rod separated the living room from the bedroom.

Father finally told them to go play on the swings. Previous owners had left a set with a wooden frame. It stood on unanchored triangular bases in the backyard. The frame would lift off the ground if they went too high.

Father had warned them about tipping over. When Marcia wanted to see how high too high was, Lee Ann began to shriek

"All right you sissy, I won't go any higher."

They were so happy. It seemed that it had been a long time since they had been in a home with both parents. They played in the yard until dark.

Marcia had wanted to explore the vacant lot beyond the chain link fence, but Louis told them to stay in the yard. She was satisfied for the moment.

Mother supervised their baths. She seemed to be thinking of something else and her eyes were very sad. Occasionally a tear would trickle down her cheek. When Lee Ann asked why Mommy was sad, Julia said she wasn't sad, just happy that they were all together again. Father tucked them in. They shared a double bed in one of the unfinished basement rooms. He kissed their foreheads. Lee Ann was asleep by the time Louis had reached the main floor.

Marcia could see through the basement window. She shifted back and forth trying to calm the restless energy that swirled within her. She had asked at dinner if it were really true that they were staying; that they would never go back. Both parents had assured the girls that they would live here with them. No more orphanage. Marcia and Lee Ann beamed. They didn't notice the somber air surrounding their parents. They were too happy. So the sisters sat at a small white table, in a sparse white kitchen, in a tiny rundown house across the street from the railroad tracks and laughed and chattered with joyful abandon. They were staying. This was heaven.

Marcia drifted off. She didn't even hear the ambulance pulling into the emergency room on the other side of the hospital. The soft breeze rustled the curtains and more pleasant thoughts occupied her dreams.

Chapter *Five*

Marcia's favorite time of year had arrived. Warm afternoons were sandwiched between cool mornings and crisp evenings. The trees were flaunting their colors. The gardener had filled the urns on the steps with rust colored mums. Most days she could get out for a late afternoon walk. Some days she walked with classmates who were also eager for a change from the classes and labs.

Judy had become Marcia's best friend and her Nursing Arts partner. Judy had always wanted to be a nurse and approached practice with tremendous seriousness. Marcia called her "Super Nurse", but was relieved to find that Judy was so skilled, especially when they were practicing injections on each other. One morning as they were crossing Franklin Street to the Nursing Arts building, an older brick home that the hospital had purchased, Judy spoke.

"I heard that Ginny's partner stuck her eight times before she got it right. You'd better give me a good shot on the first try or I'll slug you and since we're partners, I'll figure out something else to do to you."

"I'll do my best," Marcia grinned.

"I don't know how you learn anything. You're always dozing off in class."

"I don't always doze off, just after lunch," Marcia protested. "The classrooms get so warm that I can't stay awake. Yesterday Flo pinched me until my arm was black and blue, and even that didn't help. Maybe I should volunteer to be the practice dummy. Then I could lie down and sleep; besides, those mannequins are looking pretty ratty," Marcia laughed.

"You'll wish you were the dummy if you don't pass that big exam coming up in chemistry. You have zero notes. You can copy mine if you'd like."

"I don't want to take your notes. You need to study them yourself. I'll be fine. I'll just review the texts and workbooks."

Marcia didn't get slugged nor did she fail her exam. She had done well on the quizzes and after six weeks of training, both she and Judy were in the top fifth of their class. Still, Judy still couldn't help chiding Marcia for her seemingly casual attitude toward their studies. Marcia enjoyed being a student. She could spend hours in a classroom as long as it didn't involve sitting for a lecture after lunch.

Marcia's mind was not entirely on studies. They were going to have a dance. The invitations had been sent to several male colleges in the area. She was nervous. Although she would not vocalize it, she didn't place as much importance on graduating as she did on getting married. She badly wanted a home of her own and a solid, happy marriage, but was as yet unaware of her possible deficits in producing one. She saw this dance as her first chance to find a husband. Her requirements were simple. He would need to be tall and Catholic.

She worried about her clothes. She only had two skirts and three sweaters. She hadn't yet saved enough for a new outfit. She would have to make due; after all, it was just a sock hop. The limited wardrobe would not necessarily hinder her from finding a boyfriend; someone to love her.

She remembered being at the O'Shea's. How she admired Mrs. O'Shea. They had eight children and were planning more. The house was bursting with love and a level of activity that Marcia found enjoyable. That was her goal. That was what she longed to have.

The dance finally arrived and the dorm was a flurry of activity as everyone got ready. Marcia gazed into the mirror over the sink in her room. She scowled at the image. She did not see a young woman with an attractive smile and a pretty face framed by shiny auburn hair. She had never considered herself anything but homely. She was realistic enough, however, to acknowledge that she had a remarkable figure and long well shaped legs. *Maybe the guys won't notice my face,* she thought. *The lighting will probably be dim. That will be to my advantage.* She decided not to wear her hated glasses as she could see fairly well in the daytime without them.

She pulled a gold sweater and brown skirt flecked with strands of mossy green and gold from her closet and laid them on her bed. Then she went to shower.

Jane was combing her long blonde hair when Marcia returned. "Is that what you're wearing?" Jane gestured toward the bed.

"Yes, it is."

"It'll look good on you."

"Thanks."

"Like my new outfit?"

"It's lovely." Marcia admired the soft cashmere sweater and matching green wool skirt. "You'll look stunning," she said truthfully.

"I only wish I had some decent shoes," Jane whined.

Marcia was astonished. "You mean one of your thirty pair won't work?"

Marcia tried to make the observation lightly, but she was amazed that Jane, who had an overflowing closet and chest of drawers and heaps of apparel stuffed under her bed, could find anything to complain about. Marcia had one pair of heels, a pair of flats, her nursing oxfords, and a pair of tennis shoes. If she counted her slippers with the holes in both toes, she could claim five pair of shoes.

She took her turn in front of the mirror to apply mascara and lipstick.

"Aren't you going to wear any make-up?"

"I am."

"No, I mean foundation, powder, blush."

"I just wear lipstick and mascara."

"Oh. I thought you were just doing that 'cause of classes." Jane eyed her, "What perfume are you going to wear?"

Marcia colored slightly. "I don't own any."

"You don't?" Jane was the astonished one. "I'll give you some of mine. Come see what smells the best to you." Jane began to rummage through a large cosmetic case crammed with bottles of all colors and shapes. Marcia shook her head to refuse, but Jane was insistent.

"You need to wear something. Here take this. I don't smell good in Chanel. Take it!" Jane picked up Marcia's hand and shoved the bottle into it. Before Marcia could say a word, Jane was out the door.

"See you at the dance," she called over her shoulder.

Marcia wondered why Jane would buy expensive perfume that she didn't even like. Then she remembered that she had heard rumors that Jane took things. Jane had so much money, why would she steal? It didn't make any sense, but then it didn't make sense that Jane cheated on exams either. She seemed very smart. After all, she did pass the entrance exams.

Marcia and her classmates had warned the instructors that they had a cheater among them, yet no one wanted to out-and-out report Jane. They watched her read answers hidden on the hems of her uniform skirt and on the white adhesive tape that she stuck on the tongues of her shoes. Marcia had to admit that Jane was very resourceful when it came to deception.

She uncapped the bottle. The fragrance was lovely. How could she accept something from someone she neither liked nor respected? And to top it off, the gift might be stolen. She knew Jane wouldn't take it back. She had watched Jane throw beautiful new things into the trash, things others had refused to accept when she tried to give them away.

Marcia placed a few drops behind her ears and carefully placed the bottle in her drawer. She would discuss this with Judy later. Right now she needed to get down to the dance.

Chapter *Six*

The jukebox shimmered from the corner of the rec. room. "Theme to a Summer Place," one of Marcia's favorites, was the background music for the few couples who were dancing. Most of the guys stood along one wall and most of the student nurses were lined upon the other side. She entered with several classmates and stopped to watch the males size up each student nurse as she came through the door. Marcia soon found Judy, who was as tall as she was and easy to spot.

"How's the cattle call going? Have you met anyone?" Marcia asked.

"I got here right before you did."

Judy's soft voice was almost drowned out by "Tequila," the new record. Marcia couldn't help tapping her feet to the beat. Mary Beth, Ellen, and Flo joined them and they pulled the folding chairs into a slight curve; enough to talk, but not enough to ward off any possible dance partners.

Flo surveyed Marcia's face. "Where are your glasses?"

"Oh, I can see pretty well without them, so I left them upstairs."

"Really? So what does that guy by the far end of the refreshment table look like?"

"Well...he's short..."

"And?"

"It's a bit too dim in here. I can't really tell," Marcia reluctantly admitted.

Flo laughed. "You can't tell because you can't see. At least he's wearing his glasses."

"Men look better in glasses."

"That's just your excuse."

Honest, direct Flo. Marcia liked her even when she was the one under her scrutiny.

"Okay, I hate my glasses."

"Okay, admit it. You're vain." Now Flo was really laughing.

The conversation was interrupted when three of the group were asked to dance. Mary Beth scooted over. Mary Beth was as tiny as Jane, but didn't swear, cheat, or smoke. She was a serious student and had a pleasant voice. She was a pretty girl with sandy brown hair and brown eyes. If Marcia had to think of a single word to describe her, it was "lady".

"See that guy coming this way? I think he's going to ask you to dance," Mary Beth observed.

"He's way too short for me. I'm going to stand up and pretend to look for something behind my chair. Maybe he'll ask you."

"If he wanted to ask me, he would have. You can relax," Mary Beth suppressed a laugh. "He made a U turn in the middle of the floor. Guess we can both stay seated. Why didn't you want to dance with him?"

"Because during slow dances, really short guys have their nose in my boobs and I hate it."

The floor was becoming crowded with couples. Flo returned and Mary Beth was asked to dance.

He was almost to her chair before Marcia was aware of his presence.

"Would you care to dance?"

"I'd love to."

He looked down on her as he guided her around the floor. "I'm Greg Fisher."

"Marcia Gardinier," she smiled up at him. He was so handsome; blue eyes, a cleft chin and dimples in a strong masculine face. The receding brown hair was not a detraction. The music was a romantic ballad and he held her close. She hoped her perfume was as pleasing to him as his cologne was to her.

"Where do you go to school?"

"I'm studying business at Regis."

"Are you a senior?"

"No, I'm a freshman. I was in the military and am on the GI Bill. What year are you?"

"I'm a freshman too."

They spent the rest of the evening together, dancing and making small talk. Marcia was so utterly occupied with Greg that she took no notice of anyone else.

All too soon Mrs. Mac, the head housemother, announced the last dance.

"Can I call you?"

"Oh, yes."

They stopped in the middle of the floor as Greg retrieved a pad and pen from the inner pocket of his sport coat. Marcia gave him the number to the second floor phone booth and explained how the system worked and when they were allowed to receive calls.

"Only until eight on school nights and until ten-thirty on weekends. I'm out of class by four-thirty and usually go to supper between five-thirty and six. If you can't get through by eight the line will open again at ten, after study time. We have a half-hour between ten and ten-thirty to receive calls."

Marcia was thrilled that he took her hand as they walked up the stairs.

Both housemothers were standing in the hall leading to the main door. Greg squeezed her hand and promised to call. She watched him go down the sidewalk and then hurried upstairs.

Judy and Ellen had another of the large corner rooms which served as a gathering spot for their group. She could hear excited voices even before she reached the door. Marcia gave a quick tap and entered.

"We all got asked for our numbers. Did you?" Ellen asked. Marcia nodded and everyone cheered. Marcia had barely wedged herself onto the bed when a loud knock announced the housemother.

"Girls, it's after one and it's light out. You have all day tomorrow to talk." They all groaned.

"Back to your rooms."

"Yes, Mrs. Mac," they chorused.

Marcia changed into PJs and washed her face. Her little jar of cold cream was almost empty. She would go shopping tomorrow.

She looked at Jane's bed and realized that it appeared to have someone in it, although she couldn't hear Jane breathing as she usually could. Marcia moved closer for an inspection. The blanket and towels were skillfully rolled to resemble a body and the furry cap did look like hair from a distance. So that was why Mrs. Mac hadn't herded Jane back. She had already checked the room and thought Jane was asleep.

It was Marcia's turn to mound her pillow and blanket into a human form. She quietly cracked her door and peeked out. The door at the end of the hall was closing. The others must be returning to Judy's. She started down the hall. If she ran into either of the housemothers, she'd say she was on her way to the bathroom.

She didn't take time to tap, just opened the door and slipped inside. Ten girls were perched on the beds and window ledges. They were passing around paper cups.

"Carole got one of the punch buckets past the chaperones. Want some?" Marcia nodded.

"Any cookies?"

"No such luck," Carole said.

Everyone talked about their potential boyfriends. They seemed pleased with the outcome of the first dance.

"Did you see that guy your roomy was with?" Ellen asked Marcia. "He seemed bombed. They left the dance early."

"If you ask me, I think Jane had something too. She was acting spacey and smelled like booze when she talked," Judy added. "I'm surprised the chaperones didn't notice how wobbly she was."

"Well, I can't tell you anything. Jane's not in our room. She's probably hiding out with Marianne. Maybe they'll catch her drinking. They don't seem to be able to catch her cheating," Marcia observed. "I haven't seen any signs of booze in the room; but I'm sure not going to go through her rat's nest of a closet." A few girls nodded in agreement.

Marcia groaned as a new thought struck her.

"What's wrong with you? I thought you just met Prince Charming," Flo said.

"I forgot I promised Dr. Henry that I'd babysit for him next Friday. What if Greg asks me out?"

"You'll have to tell him Saturday or Sunday."

"I work on Sunday afternoons and we have to be in by eight. It would be a really short date. Anyone want to sit on Friday? They have nice kids and they pay fifty cents an hour, double what the other residents pay." There were no takers so Marcia contented herself with the prospect of at least two dollars and hopes for a Saturday date.

After they had discussed every aspect of the evening, she returned to her room. Jane was still missing. Marcia was delighted to have the space to herself.

It was ten the next morning before Jane returned to the room. She waved feebly as she headed to her bed. She kicked off her heels, dumped the rolled up towels onto the floor, flopped down and pulled the covers over head. Marcia guessed that she went to sleep immediately. She hadn't even taken off her beautiful new outfit.

Chapter *Seven*

Late Saturday morning, Marcia and her friends took the bus downtown. She purchased the items on her list and then looked at clothes. She didn't try any on, but was happy to help the others make a choice. They stopped at a soda fountain and Marcia ordered a green river, her favorite lemon-lime concoction. She had a feeling of well being as she walked along. She had been able to pay for her things without adding the sum in her head before approaching the register, and she was able to splurge on a drink. It had been a perfect day.

As they entered the lobby, Mrs. Jones called, "Miss Gardinier, you had a call from home."

Marcia had written one note to her mother and had called her twice since her arrival. She hadn't meant to ignore her mother and sister, but she was enjoying the separation from them and had little she wanted to share with her mother. She went to the phone booth as soon as she had deposited her bags on the bed. Jane was still sleeping. Marcia had counted out enough change for a fifteen minute call. She would update her mother on her classes and let her know that she was now working, and Julia wouldn't need to send any money, not that Julia had. She hadn't even mentioned Marcia's finances.

The call lasted ten minutes. Most of the conversation was about her sisters. Marcia had to frequently remind Julia that Lee Ann was no longer her responsibility or under her control and could ignore any suggestions or demands Julia made.

"Mom, she sees it as meddling."

"Well, I'm only trying to help her; to get her to do what's best."

"I think you're a bit late."

"Well, what do I do about Collette?"

Marcia sighed and gave her mother some short, but explicit directions which she knew would be forgotten as soon as Julia hung up the receiver. Julia frequently cried or whimpered when she complained. Marcia had the feeling that her mother liked being caught up in some type of drama, even if she had to manufacture it.

Marcia had Julia repeat the instructions she had given and added , "Remember, you're the parent."

"I know," Julia whimpered, "it's just so hard."

"Well, it might be a bit easier if you took some of my suggestions."

The conversation ended shortly after that.

Marcia decided to go for a walk. She felt the usual frustration she had when she talked with her mother. She knew she had to do better. She could not let Julia annoy her so. Marcia knew she had little tolerance for Julia and hated that she always felt like the adult when dealing with her. *She's my mother. She gave me the gift of life. I owe her for that.*

As she signed out, Mrs. Jones asked if she was feeling alright. Her face must still have been flushed.

"I'm fine. Thanks for asking." Marcia headed out the door.

The slight breeze and warm afternoon sun soothed her. Marcia thought about her mother. She didn't remember ever feeling that warm closeness she supposed other mothers and daughters had. As she had gotten older, Marcia told herself that her mother loved her and her sisters as best she could in her own way, but feeling close or sharing intimate parts of her life were not part of their relationship. Too much had happened to let Marcia depend on her mother for emotional support. But there had been a few times when she was younger.....

Mother had said she would come to her Brownie Christmas program before she went to work. The church basement was filling and there was still no sign of her. Marcia was relieved. Her leaders were giving the troop last minute instructions. Marcia loved both of her leaders, but Mrs. Eastland was her favorite. Her voice was soft. She wore little make-up and sometimes she came to meetings in a suit and heels. Her shoulder length hair was neatly tucked behind her ears revealing small pearl earrings. She moved with a stately grace that Marcia admired. Marcia noticed a faint, pleasant fragrance whenever she stood next to Mrs. Eastland.

Mrs. Nichols moved to the doors to welcome arriving parents. Above the hum of the crowd, Marcia heard Julia. She was greeting Mrs. Nichols. Marcia was embarrassed for her mother.

The girls had been instructed to greet their parents when they arrived and escort them to a seat. Marcia hesitated on the stage adjusting the belt on her uniform. Her mother's white rayon uniform seemed brighter than usual and her heavy make-up, like her loud voice, was noticeable across the room.

She's my mom and she did come, Marcia chided herself. She walked down the stairs and went to greet her mother. Julia gave her a big smile and bent down to kiss her cheek. Marcia could smell the Clove gum her mother used to freshen her breath. As usual her clothes smelled like cigarettes and heavy perfume, but nothing, gum or perfume, could hide the stale smoke smell.

Julia whispered, "Like my new hankie?" She pointed to the purple and white flowered handkerchief fan-folded across her left shoulder and held in place by a pearl hatpin. Marcia nodded. Her mother took a seat on the aisle in the last row. Marcia gratefully rejoined the others on the stage.

Mrs. Eastland blew the pitch pipe and the girls began to sing. Marcia noticed Julia leave halfway through the last song. She felt a guilty relief that her mother would not be mingling with the other parents when they had cookies and punch. Nevertheless, tomorrow morning when she saw her mother, she would thank her for coming. She knew that cabs weren't cheap and that Mother had to come out of her way to attend the program.

Mrs. Nichols and Mrs. Eastland had baked beautiful cookies and arranged them on doily-covered trays, the likes of which Marcia had never seen. She thought this was grand. The cookies were delicious. When Marcia returned to the table a third time, Mrs. Nichols gently put her hand on her shoulder and whispered for her to wait until everyone had gotten a chance for seconds.

"Oh, okay." Marcia had not considered this. She was anxious to please her leaders and went off to play with the others. The etiquette lesson had not been wasted. Marcia thought about it as she walked home. Her parents had taught her and her sisters to say "please" and "thank you" and sometimes admonished that they should "wait your turn," but Marcia was starting to realize that she needed to be more observant. She could learn to improve her manners.

Chapter *Eight*

Marcia kicked the leaves. She liked the crunch. She circled the park and started back to the dorm.

Before they had bikes, she and Lee Ann walked everywhere.

The week after they moved to Midwest Avenue they went exploring. Dad was at work and Mom certainly didn't care. She was avidly reading the latest True Confessions and barely looked up as they left. They weren't to cross any streets, but that didn't mean they couldn't go around the block.

Their house was the second of three identical structures, only the others were much better kept. An alley separated the houses from the blacksmith's. They watched as the smithy shoed a big brown horse. He greeted the girls and returned to his work. He would try the shoe on the hoof and then grasp it with long tongs and put it back over the bright coals. He would hammer the shoe and dunk it in a nearby barrel of water. It took numerous times before he was satisfied with the results. Several times he wiped his sweaty forehead with a dirty leather apron. The girls were fascinated.

"I want a horse," said Lee Ann as they left.

"What? Where would you keep it and what would it eat?"

"We could keep it in that other room in the basement and I could bring it lots of grass," said Lee Ann hopefully.

"What a dummy you are! A horse could never get up and down those stairs and they eat more than grass. We can't afford one."

Lee Ann seemed undaunted. She would ask mom. Mother had a horse when she was a girl. Maybe they could move to a ranch.

The low adobe house on the corner was almost hidden by weeds and overgrown bushes. The girls turned the corner and curiously observed a clump of tiny brown cabins with tar paper roofs. They were perched on concrete blocks. A grizzled old man came to the door of the nearest cabin and threw a basin of soapy water on the dirt. He gave them an almost toothless smile. His few remaining teeth glistened a golden brown. The breeze ruffled his scant gray hair.

"Morn'n gerls."

They returned his greeting. Marcia felt Lee Ann's hand steal into hers. They resumed walking. Marcia led Lee Ann past two long gray apartment buildings and another vacant weed-filled lot. An old cottonwood stood at the edge of the lot. The leaves on the remaining few branches fluttered merrily in the breeze. Only one house remained before they were on the corner of Yellowstone Highway and Spruce. Marcia was delighted to see that the building next to the house was a market. Perhaps they could come shopping with their parents. As they passed the small brown building that housed Murray's Market, Lee Ann began to tug on Marcia's hand.

"We're too far away from home."

"No, we're not. We haven't even got 'round our block, you Ninny!"

"Dad said we should play in the yard," Lee Ann remonstrated.

Marcia scowled at her sister.

"Come on. We'll start home. We'll never have friends if we always stay in the yard."

The trip toward home produced two more vacant lots and a few houses. One of them had bicycles on the sidewalk in front of it. Perhaps they would find friends there. No children were visible, but they could hear screaming and profanity coming from the open windows of a whitewashed building that appeared to have been a former place of business. These were children's voices. Marcia was pleased. There were other kids around and plenty of places to play.

Cheerful music and the sound of clicking almost drowned out the fighting as they approached the corner. The door to a dance studio was open and they could see a row of girls in colorful costumes skillfully tapping to the music. The instructor was walking back and forth counting time.

"Maybe we could learn to tap," Lee Ann ventured hopefully.

"Maybe."

At the house next to theirs an old woman in a cotton housedress with a patterned scarf on her head was pulling weeds. Her yard was full of beautiful flowers and smooth green grass. The steps were covered with pots of varied sizes and colors. Flowers and brightly leafed plants spilled over their rims. She looked up as they passed.

"Are you girls from next door?"

"Yes Ma'am. We just moved in."

"Where you from?"

Marcia was quick to answer, "Oh we lived in another part of Casper. I'm Marcia and this is Lee Ann."

"I'm Mrs. Weaver," she smiled pleasantly. "Do you girls like flowers?"

"OH YES!"

Mrs. Weaver snipped several stems and handed them to Lee Ann.

"Have your mother put them in a vase."

The girls thanked her and ran toward the house. The carpool bringing father home arrived at the gate just as they did. They showed him the bouquet.

He called to Mrs. Weaver, "Thank you for the flowers. I hope the girls weren't bothering you."

"Oh no," she smiled, "it was nice to meet them."

As they entered the house they began to talk about the afternoon's great expedition.

Lee Ann proudly presented Julia with the flowers. "Aren't they pretty?" she beamed.

"Yes they are," Julia nodded.

"You girls go play on the swing. Julia, I'd like a word with you."

Lee Ann went to the swings while Marcia crept under the window.

They were arguing again. Louis did not want the girls out of the yard by themselves.

"Louis, Marcia will be walking to school. That means she'll be leaving the yard. It's over a mile and she'll have to cross the tracks. She will eventually walk by herself. I can't drag Lee Ann every day. She still needs an occasional nap and I don't feel well."

"Well you should accompany her as much as you can. I don't want her walking through the tracks. Teach her to use Ash Street. There's a stoplight and sidewalks there."

"That's a lot longer. It's really out of the way. School lets out at four-thirty. In the winter it will be quite dark by the time she gets home."

Louis was undeterred. "I still think it's much safer. You will do as I say and teach her to use Ash." Julia said nothing and started for the pantry.

After dinner Louis settled into the armchair.

"Come here girls. I need to talk to you." It was the perfect bedtime tale. Louis gave detailed descriptions of those unfortunate children who had been hit by trains while playing on the tracks or by climbing under apparently stopped boxcars.

"Those trains can start up at any time. You are NEVER to climb on or under the cars. Do you understand?" The girls nodded solemnly. Lee Ann's eyes were wide with fright.

Louis was still not assured that he had given an adequate warning of the impending dangers they might face. He launched into a description of the fate awaiting poor creatures that fell into the lye pit across the street by the tanks. It was a large hole surrounded by a rickety sign covered fence.

"Terrible, painful burns," he intoned. "The lye can eat off feathers, fur or skin. You do not want to go near the lye pit. Don't even climb on the fence. It's old and if it collapsed, you could fall in."

One last caution remained. They were to stay away from all the men who rode in the boxcars and anyone else wandering through the tracks. They gave him a somber promise to heed his warnings.

"I love you girls and just want you to be safe," he concluded.

After he had tucked them in and gone upstairs, Lee Ann whispered, "Are the people here going to hurt us?"

"No. Dad is trying to scare us so we don't get hurt. We left the mean people at the Children's Home. The lady next door seems real nice, huh?"

Lee Ann agreed. She rolled over and was soon fast asleep.

Chapter *Nine*

School had started. Marcia had two new dresses, a corduroy jumper with a pretty long sleeved cotton blouse, and a pair of sturdy brown oxfords. Father had taken her downtown to the expensive shoe store. The store had an x-ray machine with three eye ports that customers could peer in and see if their shoes fit properly. Marcia's feet were bathed in green light. It was fascinating to see all the bones in her feet. The clerk hit the button a second time so Marcia could again look at her feet in the shiny new shoes. Father said that shoes needed to fit because, "If your feet hurt your whole body hurts." To save money his family had worn shoes in the winter only. When the school year started, the shoes were passed down to the next child. Only the oldest boy and girl had new shoes. Louis had told them that many times his feet hurt and were covered with blisters.

Louis did not give clothing the same high esteem he gave to shoes. This resulted in fierce battles with Julia over the girls' wardrobes. Julia had been raised in a poor ranching family. She and her sisters had to wear their brother's outgrown overalls and had little feminine clothing. She detested anything denim and swore her daughters would never wear it in any form. She looked for flowered prints, colors she considered feminine, and anything with lace. She was not inclined to pick "serviceable" over pretty for any amount of savings.

The first few days mother walked the Ash Street route with her. They were the only ones walking to the intersection. All the neighborhood kids cut through the tracks. The fourth day Marcia assured Julia that she knew the way. Julia gave her a brown paper bag and kissed her on the cheek.

"I believe you do know the way." Her mother watched from the porch until Marcia reached the corner. Her best friend Sally was walking toward Midwest with her older sister. Marcia waved and waited.

"Where's your mom and sister?"

"They're not coming. Can I walk with you?"

"I thought you had to take the intersection."

"Well, the tracks are much shorter."

"If your dad finds out, you'll get in trouble."

"I'm not worried. I'm not afraid of my father," replied a defiant Marcia.

"Oh yes you are."

Marcia and Sally stayed near the bigger kids as they crossed the tracks, but they gave themselves a little distance so Sally could complain about her mean older brother. It was Sally's family that lived in the converted store, and it was Sally and her older brother Henry who were screaming and swearing at each other the day Marcia and LeeAnn had walked by. Sally's father had died. He had been seeing another woman and they were together when the car overturned, killing them both. Mrs. Boland had been devastated. Now she worked as a waitress to support her family. This unsupervised time enabled Henry to do as he liked, which usually included making life miserable for his sisters, especially Sally. Marcia wasn't sure who Sally hated most, her deceased father or her brother.

"You'd better keep up or a train will roll right over your ugly faces." Henry taunted.

"Oh shut up. We're fine," Sally hollered.

Marcia thought the kindergarten classroom was the best place she had ever been. The playhouse had dress up clothes, hats and purses. It had a small blue table and chairs and a cabinet filled with miniature dishes. The windows in the walls of the playhouse had lovely white gauze curtains.

There were easels and shelves of books. Miss Goddard read to them every day. Marcia loved Miss Goddard even though her teacher was continually telling her to speak softly, raise her hand, take her turn, and sit still. Marcia was quite happy there.

It didn't seem that it had been too long after she started school that she heard her parents talking about a baby. She had come upstairs for a drink.

She heard the news with trepidation. The last time she had heard talk of an expected baby, she had been sitting quietly under a kitchen table, hidden by a long checkered oilcloth. Her mother was discussing something with Alvan, who had become a frequent visitor while her father was away serving his country. Something important was being discussed because they talked in hushed voices. She clutched her long legs tightly to her chest. She hardly breathed. She strained to hear.

Julia was ironing. Marcia watched her mother's feet shift as she ironed. Alvan was drinking coffee. His crossed legs were inches from Marcia's face.

"He should be here in two weeks," Julia said nervously.

"I'll be with you," he replied. "Everything will be alright. Are you pretty well packed up?"

Her mother said that she was and they started talking about the ranch. Julia was happy to return to country life.

"I think the girls will love it. They can learn to ride." Mother stopped swaying.

"I'm so tired and my back hurts. I just want this over."

"Our little guy will be here soon and we'll all be on the ranch. Just think how good life will be. You'll be away from this neighborhood. No more break-ins, no murders. Just be patient."

It was time for Alvan to leave. Marcia left her hiding place when her mother accompanied him to the door.

Julia seemed increasingly distraught as the next days passed.

Father's unit did return from Japan and he did come back to the house, but she and Lee Ann did not accompany their mother and Alvan to the ranch. Their mother was crying as she left with Alvan.

"Look, I have something for each of you." Julia's hand was shaking as she reached for a big brown bag.

"New dolls. Aren't they pretty?" She gave one to each girl and kissed them on the cheek, and then she was gone.

A week later a stern looking lady came to the house. She took them to a big black car which was waiting by the curb. Louis cried as he knelt down and hugged the girls.

"This won't be long, I promise. I'll find a job and get us a place to live."

They were placed in the back with the woman while a man in a uniform drove them away.

Lee Ann bent over her doll and tenderly kissed her cheek. Marcia's doll sat unnoticed in her lap.

It seemed like a very long time before they passed through the wrought iron gates and turned up a gently sloping hill. The car stopped in front of a three story brick building and they were told to get out. Another stern looking woman greeted their companion. Marcia heard them exchange whispers about these newest girls having an unfit mother who cheated on her serviceman husband.

They were taken to a room with two rows of beds on its longest sides. Each bed had its own little foot locker. The suitcase containing their clothes disappeared.

"Give me those dolls."

Before their owners could protest, the dolls were confiscated and disappeared with the suitcase. A bewildered Lee Ann began to wail.

The second stern looking woman grabbed Lee Ann's arm and began to shake her.

"You stop that nonsense! RIGHT NOW!" her voice was low and threatening.

Lee Ann's eyes widened with surprise. She reached toward Marcia as she gulped to control her sobs.

An older grandmotherly looking woman entered the room at that moment.

"I'm here this evening. I'll be glad to settle them in."

Miss Brown flung Lee Ann's arm down and walked to the door. She stopped at the doorway and hissed at the older woman, "You are way too soft on these brats!"

It was hard to sleep. The mattress was lumpy and the hall lights shone through the transoms. Marcia's eyes burned and the lump in her throat hurt. She wondered where their clothes and the new dolls were.

Why did mom have to leave with Alvan? Why couldn't they go live on the ranch with their mother and father?

Chapter *Ten*

Miss Brown had decided that since the sun was shining, the children needed to get some fresh air. There was little snow on the playground, but the children were not playing. They were huddled near a stand of pines that acted as a wind break from the face-numbing Wyoming wind. Evidently Miss Brown did not need any fresh air herself as she only watched them from her window. An older girl, one of the "privileged" who were chosen to learn secretarial skills in the office, approached the shivering group. She gestured to Marcia and Lee Ann.

"You need to come with me."

The three tucked their heads down and bent into the wind as they headed towards the building. Once inside the entrance hall they stamped their feet on the mat and gratefully inhaled the warm air. Marcia and Lee Ann worked their numb fingers open and shut to regain the circulation.

"You're wanted in the parlor," the older girl said as she pointed to a small room near the office.

Julia was waiting for them. Lee Ann squealed with delight and before Julia could rise from the couch, Lee Ann was in her lap. Marcia trotted to her mother and after a hug and kiss sat next to her. Julia talked quietly. She rarely had feelings of remorse, so she was ill prepared for the intensity of the emotions she had when she looked at the peaked faces of her children. She asked about the food, their daily activities, and if they had made friends. Marcia answered cautiously while Lee Ann sat with her head against her mother's bosom and fingered the buttons on her blouse.

"I bought you something for Christmas. They wouldn't let me bring anything pretty. I see you're not even wearing your own clothes."

Marcia explained that all clothing was kept in a storeroom between the dorms.

"They marked our clothing when we came. Sometimes we get our own and sometimes not. Depends on where you are in line when they hand out clothes. See, I have Hazel James' dress today," Marcia shifted to show her mother the tag on the collar.

The presents were new socks and underwear. Julia had also purchased a flowered print gown for each girl. Marcia wondered if she would be the first one to wear her gown.

"Can't we come home?" Marcia implored. "We don't like it here."

Julia slowly shook her head. "Not right now."

Marcia suddenly remembered that mother was supposed to have a baby.

"Do we have a brother or a sister?"

"You have a sister and her name is Olivia."

"What does she look like? Can we see her?" both girls asked.

"She's beautiful, but I don't think we should talk about her anymore." Julia's eyes were filling with tears.

"Why can't we see her?" The girls were puzzled.

Julia sighed heavily. She stood and placed Lee Ann on the couch.

"It's time for me to go. You be good. I love you." Mother's voice was husky. She left quickly.

Evidently everyone had gotten enough fresh air, so the girl from the office took them to join the others in the playroom. Even the bright sun pouring through the windows gave Marcia no comfort that day.

The austere surroundings were altered by the presence of a towering Christmas tree in the front hall. The children passed it every time they went to the dining room. Marcia thought it was beautiful. The sparkling ornaments and long strings of tinsel made her happy. One night the high school choir came to sing. The words in the carols soothed Marcia. They spoke to her of love and hope. She was sorry when the program ended, even if it meant a trip to the dining room for hot Ovaltine and a cookie.

Two days before Christmas, Marcia and Lee Ann were called from the playroom. One of the caretakers gave each girl a brown bag partially filled with clothing. On the top Marcia recognized mother's Christmas present, her flowered nightgown. Lee Ann had hers also.

"Come girls."

This time their father was waiting in the parlor. "Daddy!" both exclaimed.

Marcia hugged him around his waist while Lee Ann attached herself to one of his legs. Miss Brown was explaining something about time and their father was saying he understood.

"How about you girls coming with me?" Their yesses were unrestrained.

As soon as they were in the taxi, Marcia asked, "Are we leaving this place?"

"You get to spend a whole week with me," Louis replied with the utmost cheerfulness he could muster.

Marcia was suddenly solemn. A sick feeling filled her stomach. She sat next to her father with her head resting on his arm. Their destination was a small rundown hotel. The halls seemed very dark compared with the bright halls of the orphanage. Even in the dimness, the peeling paint on the walls was visible.

They had meals at a nearby café and took short walks to town where they could window shop. One afternoon he took them to the Rialto. The theater was having a Christmas party. Not only was there a double feature and news reel, but they had two cartoons. As they exited, all children under twelve received a brown bag half full of popcorn and peanuts and two pieces of brightly colored ribbon candy. The girls ignored their father's suggestion that they save some of the contents for later and devoured all of it as they walked back to the hotel.

Most of the time, however, was spent at one of the tables in the hotel's shabby lobby. Louis had purchased Chutes and Ladders and they passed the hours playing the game. When Louis read the paper, the girls looked at the pictures in the worn copies of *The Saturday Evening Post* and *Life* that lay around the lobby. They all slept in the double bed in his tiny room. Marcia felt safe sleeping near her father and her sleep was sounder than it had been for months.

The visit passed much too quickly for the girls. As the cab neared the big wrought iron gates on the trip back, Lee Ann began to cry.

"Daddy, don't leave us. We'll be good. We'll be good."

"You are good, Sweetheart. You're both good," Louis murmured as he patted her hair.

"Then why can't we stay with you?"

"Pretty soon you can. I have a job now. Pretty soon."

Lee Ann was still whimpering when they reached the stairs. As they waited for the door to open, Marcia leaned close and whispered, "Stop crying or you'll get in trouble."

A look of fear crossed Lee Ann's face and she stopped crying immediately.

Miss Brown answered the door. "Come in girls," she simpered. She exchanged pleasantries with Louis. When the door closed she propelled the girls toward the stairs.

"You are to get ready for bed and you are NOT to talk about your visit with your father. Do you understand? You still have both parents and have been given a privilege many of the others will never get. Don't hurt their feelings by talking about your visit. Do you understand me?" she repeated. They nodded silently.

It was a relief to see Mrs. Murphy in the dorm. She waited until Miss Brown was out of sight and then greeted them warmly.

"Did you have a good visit?" She listened as she helped them wash up and change into nightgowns. She brushed their hair and tucked them in.

"Thank you, Mrs. Murphy." Marcia smiled at her.

"You're welcome dear."

The others were filing in. Mrs. Murphy's attention turned to them. Lee

Ann, who slept in the next bed, propped herself on her elbow. "I want to go home. When can we go home?"

"I don't know. Lie down before you get into trouble."

It was almost time for the lights to go out when they heard it. A fearful hush fell and the few children still up scurried to their beds. The boy's screams could be heard over the sound of the paddle's thud. Eventually, the only sound was sobbing. Suddenly, Miss Brown, accompanied by a large woman who had a small boy draped over one arm, appeared at the door.

Mrs. Murphy hurried to them.

"Charlene, some of the children have just gone to sleep."

Miss Brown was undeterred.

"These children need to learn what happens when they disobey!"

She and her companion pushed past Mrs. Murphy. She stopped at the beds nearest the main door. With a flourish she pulled the boy's pajama pants around his legs exposing his very red buttocks.

"You are all to feel his butt. I want you to know what happens to sassy, disobedient children."

They started around the room. Marcia pushed her head into her pillow and feigned sleep. She was not touching anyone's butt. Momentarily the trio stopped at the foot of her bed and then passed on to the next child. Marcia waited and then shifted slightly. She opened her eyes a crack and surveyed the room from under the barely open lids. Miss Brown's fury had waned and Bobby was being sent to bed. Marcia could see his forlorn, tear-stained face and she felt a wave of pity for him.

Marcia's fifth birthday arrived. That morning she and several others were awakened early. They were told to dress quietly so as not to wake those still sleeping. Marcia wanted a drink, but was told to wait. All the bathroom faucets and drinking fountains had rags knotted around the spouts. The sleepy group was herded into the black sedan. It was dark and starting to snow. The wind was blowing the fragile flakes with an unwavering fierceness.

"Where are we going?" a boy asked.

"You'll soon see. Just sit quietly," came the reply.

The children were unloaded in front of a brightly lit brick building and were guided into the lobby. Mrs. Clark had them form a line in front of a lady seated at a massive brown desk. As each child approached the desk, Mrs. Clark gave information to the clerk who typed it down. Then two nurses led the children away. Marcia was placed in a white metal crib.

"I'm too old for a crib. I sleep in a bed."

"Well you'll be in a crib while you're here. Now let me help you with this gown."

"Why am I in the hospital? I'm not sick."

"You're old enough to have your tonsils out. Now sit down and be quiet."

"What are tonsils? Where are they?" Marcia's questions went unanswered as the nurse had walked away.

Soon she was rolled down a long corridor and into the strangest room she'd ever seen. Everyone was wearing dresses. All heads were covered with hats and all faces with masks. She was lifted to another bed. Before she was even settled a hard black cup was placed over her nose and mouth and a pungent odor filled her airways. She was falling down a dark chute. She tried to scream. She reached out to break her fall. "Her hands, someone grab her hands!"

Father was leaning over the crib rail when she awakened. "How's your throat?"

"Hurts," she whispered.

A few days later the black car brought everyone back from the hospital. They all returned to the dorms except one girl who was sent to the infirmary.

Lee Ann was overjoyed to see her sister. "I thought you left me!" she cried.

"No they took out my tonsils. They took us to the hospital. I would never leave you. I'll always stay with you, Lee Ann." Marcia hugged her reassuringly.

They talked about the hospital. "Were they mean to you?"

"No, most everybody was nice, but they made me sleep in a crib and wear a nightgown that isn't sewed all the way shut so your butt hangs out." Lee Ann giggled.

"My throat's sore," Marcia continued, "they take tonsils out of your throat."

"Why?"

"I don't know. I guess they wear out early."

Father came for Easter. He looked happy. "You girls are going to be coming home."

"Now? Should we get our clothes?" They pranced around him.

"I can't take you today. We still have some paperwork to finish and some things to work out."

"What papers? Who's we?" asked Marcia as she stopped dancing.

"Your mother and me."

"We're going home with you and mom?" A slender ray of hope pierced Marcia's heart.

"And Olivia? She's coming too?

Her father frowned. "It will be just you and Lee Ann."

He saw the puzzled looks and said firmly, "We don't need to talk about the baby anymore."

There was a note of finality in her father's voice that forbade any more questions about Olivia. The girls would be adults before they learned that the one child had been the ransom for her sisters' freedom. Olivia would grow up with her father on the ranch and Julia was forced to promise never to see her again. She would remarry Louis to regain the daughters she knew and loved while leaving behind the beloved she was learning to know.

The girls quickly switched to a more pressing question. "When do we get to come home?"

"In about a week."

It was the longest week ever. Now, Marcia sat on the sill of an open third floor window. A soft breeze ruffled the curtains and sunlight streamed into the room. She was watching the drive for the cab which would bring her parents. When it finally came, only her father got out and came up the walk. She thought she saw her mother sitting in the back seat. Children ran toward him from every direction. They reached for his hands and clamored for his attention. He stopped to talk with them.

"Daddy! Daddy! I'm up here!" Marcia called out the window. She waved happily. He smiled and returned her wave.

Marcia felt a painful grip on her shoulder. Miss Brown was behind her.

"You don't need to be hollering out the window. Leave those other children have time with your father. Some of them have no parents at all. You needn't be so selfish. You can share."

Marcia felt a surge of anger rising inside her. *Miss Brown was wrong! That was her father and she did not have to share! She didn't care about the others.*

Marcia dug her nails into her palms and clenched her teeth. She glanced out the window. She couldn't see her father anymore. He must be inside. He was taking them home. Miss Brown could not hurt them anymore.

Miss Brown was not accustomed to defiance nor was she prepared for the force the child used to tear away from her. Her shock had barely registered as Marcia streaked through the door.

"I don't have to listen to you anymore." Marcia disappeared down the hall.

Marcia was standing close to her father when Miss Brown reached the parlor. The defiant child glared at her from the safety of her fortress. Lee Ann was fetched from the playroom by an older girl.

"Where's mom?" Lee Ann looked around the room.

"She's waiting for you in the cab."

Father signed some more papers and they walked out into the glorious Wyoming day.

Chapter *Eleven*

Now her parents were talking about a new baby. Did this mean she and Lee Ann would be returned to the orphanage? Lee Ann still cried in her sleep at night. When Marcia had asked her why, Lee Ann said she had bad dreams about the mean people.

She got her drink. Her parents were seated at the kitchen table. Her father searched her face. "Is everything okay?"

"We're going to have a new baby?"

"Yes." Her mother smiled, "Would you like that?"

"Will we all live here? Together?"

"Of course we will," father assured her. "What do you think about that?"

"I guess that will be fine." Marcia shrugged her shoulders.

Lee Ann was delighted to hear the news. "I'll have someone to play with while you're at school."

It was early spring when mother went to the hospital. Father got them ready before he left for work. Lee Ann went with Mrs. Good. She was the mother of one of Lee Ann's friends. Since the Goods lived across the street from the Boland's, Marcia walked with them to Sally's and waited until it was time to walk to school. She was glad that her mother would soon return and she wouldn't have to wait at Sally's as Henry teased her and Sally unmercifully.

After what seemed like a very long time, mother was home. The new baby was a girl and was named Collette. They had a few visitors who declared that she was absolutely beautiful. All Marcia could see were two big brown eyes in a very red face. The baby's head was covered with little black ringlets. Marcia thought she cried a lot. Lee Ann spent hours watching Collette sleep and softly caressed the tiny hands.

The school year was ending. Father had found work with the railroad. Marcia and Sally were now quite confident walking to and from school. One day, as they were returning from school, they spotted an approaching pump car and waited for it to pass. A booming voice made both girls jump. It came from Mr. Gardinier. He was part of the work crew on the car.

"What are you girls doing on the tracks?"

"Just walking home from school, Dad."

"You get right home, you understand?"

"Yes sir."

They could see the other men on the car grinning. As soon as the orange car was out of hearing range, Sally began to fume.

"We weren't doing anything wrong. Why the hell did your dad hafta yell at us?"

"He didn't know I was cutting through the tracks. He told me not to."

"Well, that's a bunch of crap. Why shouldn't we walk this way? Men are nothing but mean and bossy jackasses!"

Marcia kept quiet and let Sally rage. She was sure Sally placed her dad in the same ranks as Henry and Sally's own father.

Marcia knew she had an unpleasant evening awaiting her, but the anticipated event was unexpectedly short and not at all what she'd envisioned. After supper, father seated himself in the arm chair. Marcia stood in front of him. She had just explained that the tracks were so much shorter and that all the neighborhood kids took that route.

"Well if they all jumped off a bridge, would you?"

Before Marcia could answer, Julia spoke quietly.

"Louis, she is probably safer with the group than by herself."

Julia bent over the oilcloth lined basket and pulled out a tightly rolled shirt. She lit a cigarette and took a long draw. Then she picked up her iron and returned to her work. She seemed oblivious of anything but the ironing. Marcia stood very still.

Louis sat quietly for a moment.

"Alright," Louis said gruffly, "you can walk with the other kids, but if you're alone, you go by way of the crossing. I don't care if it is the long way. Understand?"

"Yes sir," Marcia replied nodding, but she knew she'd never go the long way again.

"Get ready for bed."

"Yes sir."

Marcia kissed her parents goodnight and hurriedly joined Lee Ann in the basement.

"Did you get in trouble? Are you getting a spanking?"

"No."

"Do you want to sleep back-to-back?" asked Lee Ann.

The unheated basement was still quite cool, so Marcia readily agreed. They furiously rubbed their feet to warm the cold sheets. In no time at all, they were trying to kick each other and loud "ows", "not fairs", and laughter drifted upstairs.

"You girls get to sleep!" Their father thumped on the floor.

"G'night" whispered Lee Ann.

Chapter *Twelve*

It was dinner time when Marcia returned. She headed toward the hospital cafeteria where all the students ate. St. Joseph was a teaching hospital, so there were students in radiology, physical and occupational therapy, and chaplaincy mingling with the visitors. The medical students (externs), interns, and residents ate in an adjacent room reserved for doctors. Most of this latter group were young men. They frequently left the connecting door open so they could look over the student nurses when they came to the dining room.

She joined Mary Beth in the line.

"Marcia, where were you?"

"Out for a walk."

"The Regis guys called and a bunch of us are going to a movie tonight."

"Did I get a call?" Marcia asked hesitantly.

"I think Judy took one for you."

Marcia was ecstatic. "Where is she?"

"She just went through the line."

Marcia's heart was thumping. Greg had called. Life couldn't be any better.

Her blissful meditation was interrupted by Mary Beth. "See if they're hiding anything good under the counter."

They were standing next to a wall of aluminum carts which stored the extra hot and cold foods prepared for each meal. A secondary result of the wall was the restricted view of the servers and any food they might have hidden. Only the tallest students could see over the carts. Once around the corner, the shelves under the serving tables were out of sight. The better prepared and therefore, most popular items, were frequently set aside for the doctors and paying customers. The students learned that they could ask for those choices and would not be refused. The trick was in knowing what to request.

"Not tonight."

"Oh well, I'll just eat a PB&J sandwich if it's too awful," Mary Beth lamented.

They joined the others at a large circular table. Judy nodded toward an open door.

"You're in the line of scrutiny."

"Well I'm not moving to another table. Did Greg call?"

"Yes. He'll call back at eight."

"When's everyone leaving for the movies?"

"The guys are supposed to come at seven."

Marcia was intensely disappointed. The hunger from her walk disappeared. Dinner was quick. The others were anxious to get ready. Marcia wondered why Greg was calling so late. Maybe he didn't want to join the others. After all, he was older. That thought cheered her as she watched her friends leave. The phone was easy to hear on the almost deserted floor. Marcia tried to sound casual as she picked up the receiver.

Greg had car problems. He would take it into the shop on Monday when he had a break in classes. He had hoped to see her this weekend, but would she consider coffee next Sunday evening? Marcia accepted with pleasure. She reminded him that she worked until four. Greg would pick her up at six. They talked a bit longer and he was off to study.

It wasn't the date she hoped for, but it was better than no date at all.

Perhaps his car repairs were going to be costly. The thought didn't improve her mood. Now she'd be staying in most of next weekend too. Maybe some of the married residents would need a sitter. She'd put her name in the office.

Marcia returned to her room. It was so quiet. How she envied the others. She wanted to be out too. She felt a familiar vague restlessness, an emptiness filling her.

She showered, filed her nails, grabbed her novel and curled up on her bed. She was lost in her Victorian romance when her friends returned.

She joined them in Judy's room and listened half-heartedly. It was hard to pretend enthusiasm when she had been stuck at school all evening. She was not unhappy when the housemother shooed them back to their own rooms.

Chapter *Thirteen*

Marcia was content dating Greg. They did not often join the others as Greg felt many of his classmates were immature and usually he didn't enjoy their company. They spent much of their time in small cafes discussing movies they had seen, or their plans and dreams for the future.

Marcia ignored the differences in their desires and philosophies. These were "little" things that, she was sure, could be worked out. So he wanted only two children. Marcia was certain he would desire more once they started a family. So they didn't share the same devotion to the faith. She assumed that she would be able to change that also after they were married.

She was certain that she would quit school to marry Greg. She would have to quit, since the nursing students weren't allowed to marry until the last six months of training. Then she would help put him through college. She would have her PHT degree: Putting Hubby Through, everyone called it. She wasn't the least bit worried about finding a job of some type; she was a good worker. Besides, motherhood and homemaking were to be her life's work.

They went to the school sock hops and danced to all the slow, romantic ballads. Marcia was happy in his arms. She felt wanted and loved. She was going to be married and have her own home. Nothing was of greater importance.

She looked forward to the end of each date with Greg. He would find a secluded spot to park and they would spend the remainder of the evening kissing. She was careful to observe the bathing suit rule; something she had learned from her friends when they were in Judy's room discussing men and dating. She had to ask what the rule was. Everyone else seemed to know.

"It means no hands anywhere a bathing suit would touch your body," Mary Ellen explained.

"Is that a one or two piece?"

After some discussion the consensus was a two piece suit.

"Guys already touch your waist when they put their arms around you," Flo observed.

Marcia was grateful for the guideline. The only thing Julia had ever told her was that proper ladies had clean fingernails. And one night, after sitting, she stayed to talk with Mrs. Good who told her that she was making sure Regina always wore a slip.

"Ladies do not let people see through their skirts."

How they arrived on that subject, Marcia didn't remember, but she was sure there was more to lady-like behavior than clean fingernails and wearing slips.

She was not worried about premarital sex. No one in her right mind would want the stigma of an out-of-wedlock baby. Besides, most parents would kill you. Even though she wasn't close to her father, she didn't want to disappoint him in that way. To top it off, the church said sex outside of marriage was seriously wrong, a mortal sin. Marcia accepted the teaching with little thought about the theology behind it.

It seemed to be a matter of knowing the boundaries, and getting the guy interested enough to want to marry you. All it really amounted to was luring him in. Wasn't that what everyone else seemed to be doing? So why did she feel like this was the wrong approach to marriage? Why did it seem like selling oneself, just in a more covert way?

Marcia would have spent more time necking, but Greg was always quick to put a halt to things and start back to the nursing school. She would be glad when they didn't have to separate for the night.

It was surprise when Greg called mid-week during lunch break and asked if he could see her. He said it was important that they talk. He would pick her up at six. He knew she had to be in by eight and he assured her that she would be back on time. Was he finally going to ask her to marry him?

She told Judy about the call as they left the nursing arts lab.

"Why would you quit training now? You're doing great." Judy was not the least bit supportive.

"Well, maybe it's a ring. He couldn't get me anything for Valentine's Day. The car needed new tires."

"I still think it's crazy to give up training for a guy. You've got a whole lifetime ahead of you to be married. I think it's a privilege to be in this program, to be a nurse."

"Alright, alright, already! Just wish me luck. Okay?" Marcia hurried to get ready. She could talk to Judy later.

When eight-thirty had come and Marcia had not stopped by her room, Judy headed down the hall. She gave a quick knock and opened the door.

"Good grief! You look awful. What happened?"

Marcia was sitting cross-legged on her bed with a box of Kleenex in her lap and a trash can next to her. Her eyes were red and swollen. She was noisily blowing her nose. Judy sat next to her.

The words spilled out. "He broke up with me! I just don't understand! I thought things were going so well. He said we have a lot of differences and that we're getting too serious and he's not ready to be serious now and our differences will cause problems in the future. This is a fine time to decide that! We've been dating over seven months. I thought we'd be getting married." Marcia began to sob again.

"There'll be others. You'll see. Actually this is a very good time for this type of decision. Wouldn't you rather have a break-up now and not after you're married? Maybe Tom has a friend. We could double. That would be fun, wouldn't it? Think about it." Judy gave Marcia a hug.

"It will get better." Judy sat quietly with her arm around Marcia's shoulder. Gradually the crying stopped. After several minutes Judy said, "I have to go study for tomorrow's chemistry mid-term and so do you. I promise I'll talk to Tom."

"You know you sound just like a guidance counselor?" Marcia gave a wan smile. Nevertheless, the promise of another possible suitor lifted Marcia's spirits immeasurably.

"Greg can just be sorry when I find someone else," Marcia thought. She blew her nose once more and put her trash can on the floor by the desk. She began to look for her chemistry book.

Chapter *Fourteen*

Marcia enjoyed dorm life, especially now that she had a new roommate. Jane had finally been expelled, not for cheating, but for morals. She had been staying out all night on the weekends and sneaking through the tunnel connecting the school and hospital when she wanted to return the next day. One weekend, unknown to Jane, her parents were visiting friends in Denver and called the office requesting permission for Jane to have dinner with them that evening and stay overnight at the Brown.

It was an unfortunate piece of timing for Jane. She had called not five minutes earlier to say that she was with her parents at another Denver hotel and had requested and was given an "overnight" at that time. The dean of students and the director immediately called Jane's parents and requested a meeting. They would come to the Brown. The students heard rumors of what transpired. The sisters and Jane's parents went to the other hotel. Seems Jane and her boyfriend were discovered there. They were already well into an evening of partying when the good sisters and her parents knocked on the door. Why they opened the door immediately without ascertaining who the callers might be, remained a mystery.

Time in the classroom was giving way to three mornings of floor duty each week and Marcia realized she did not like many aspects of nursing. She was appalled by the havoc wreaked on the human body from accidents and disease. The smells bothered her and some of the sights made her lightheaded. Her only pleasure was the interaction with the patients. She truly liked them as people and tried to raise her mind above the immediate surroundings. While Judy returned to the classroom each afternoon elated that she could help relieve suffering, Marcia frequently returned with a sick feeling. She began to plan. She would leave the program during summer vacation. She told no one; not even Judy.

Marcia's escape was her social life. She had many blind dates, but much to her dismay, no relationship lasted. Judy and Tom broke up, but Judy didn't seem too bothered.

"Someone else will come along," she said nonchalantly.

They studied hard, but partied harder. Marcia loved to dance and could hardly wait for the weekends. Since they weren't allowed to have cars, those without dates would pile into the cars of any classmate whose date was willing, and they would head to the very popular three-two bars. In Colorado, eighteen year olds could frequent bars that served 3.2 beers, a lower alcohol version of the real drink. Less alcohol or not, imbibe enough and one could get plastered. Marcia was usually too busy dancing to consume much.

Summer vacation for Marcia was only two weeks away. She had not been scheduled for a summer rotation like her friend. She was scheduled for a break during the summer months. Marcia would go home while Judy would go for training at the psych hospital in Pueblo. In September, Judy would go home and Marcia would be assigned to more time on the surgical units. In a few days, Marcia would tell Judy about leaving and make her promise to write. Then she would tell Sister. This thought strengthened her as she worked in the wards. She was on countdown.

One noon, after they had finished their assignments and were going to lunch, Marcia was called to the office.

Now what have I done? she thought.

Perhaps Sister Albert Mary had finally heard that she was falling asleep in class. Perhaps it was about the bedpan hopper that she hadn't closed properly and the resultant flood that the torrent of water had produced in the dirty room. Marcia thought she'd cleaned it all up.

Those things are so hard to close. Why wasn't I paying attention?

Then she remembered. It was that dreamy Dr. Edward's fault. She was thinking about his cute smile. *Maybe it was about the three needles she broke when trying to sharpen them?* She'd heard a rumor that they were switching to disposable needles. Every patient would get a new needle. No more sterilizing them, checking them for burrs, or sharpening them. Well that would certainly be an improvement. But she wouldn't have to worry about that much longer. Certainly Sister didn't know she planned to leave. Her mother didn't even know that. Julia would have called Sister Albert in a fit of hysteria if she had the slightest inkling. *What could Sister possibly want with her?*

Sister Albert Mary was a large woman. She sat tall and upright in her chair. She was quite direct and came right to the point.

"Sit down, Miss Gardinier," she gestured to an armchair facing the desk. Marcia promptly sat.

"I don't know if you're aware of our alumni association."

"No, I haven't heard of it."

"Well, every year the association selects a deserving student for a one year scholarship. Your grades are excellent and we are aware of your financial need. You are the recipient for the coming year."

Marcia stared at Sister Albert in disbelief. She tried to speak. "I... Oh...A...Thank you."

"I know this is a big surprise. You are quite welcome. Congratulations. You may go now."

Marcia nodded. Her exit was a study in confusion. She tried another thank you, tripped over the foot of her chair, and ran into the door frame on her way out.

Sister Albert would say later that she had never seen a student so overwhelmed with gratitude.

Marcia had regained her senses by the time she reached her room. She was relieved that Connie, her new roommate, had already gone to lunch.

Why had she waited so long to tell Sister? Marcia felt trapped. The scholarship meant that she'd have to stay in nursing. She sat on her bed.

If I get through the second year, I might as well finish. I guess I can do anything for two years. There must be some good rotations too. It can't all be awful. I can get a job in an office when I finish. That will get me out of the wards. She felt a wave of relief as she pursued these reflections.

It was then that an amazing thought occurred to Marcia. She had just received a windfall. She had saved almost four hundred dollars. Suddenly she was rich! Now she could get contacts and get rid of her despised glasses. Now she could expand her pitiful wardrobe and, of course, she'd need to put money in savings.

She would have all year to save the two hundred needed for her senior year. She had heard that physical therapy needed an assistant for Saturday mornings and had not applied for the position. Now, since she was staying, she might see if she could work there when not away for rotation. The pay was supposed to be a dollar twenty-five an hour. She would be doing quite well if she got it. Marcia went off to lunch in a very good mood indeed.

Chapter *Fifteen*

Marcia resumed working at the bakery during vacation. Julia had been embarrassingly vocal when Marcia told her of the scholarship. The few times they were together in public, Julia would spot someone she knew and loudly announce the news. Marcia suspected that it was the attention her mother enjoyed, rather than actual pride in her daughter. She loathed these public displays.

Marcia spent little time at home. Some of her friends had returned for the summer. They would cruise Second Street with radios blaring or pack into Betty's parents' station wagon and head to the drive-in. The A&W was always a good last stop. They could look for guys while sipping on root beer floats. The expectation of meeting someone was always much higher than the reality, but it was still fun and it gave them time to talk.

With two small children, Lee Ann had scant free time. She and Marcia found little to talk about when they were together and the gap widened between them.

Marcia considered Collette the quintessential pest. She would spy from behind the living room curtains when Marcia returned from a date. She would ask her all sorts of questions about the young man, and wanted to know where they went. Collette was always at Marcia's side during the little time she was at home. Private conversation was impossible with the party line on one hand and "Little Miss Bigears" on the other. It rarely occurred to Marcia to offer her sister some attention or to take her on an outing. Collette spent much time alone with her cat. Marcia was busy with her own life.

Julia, who still worked as a waitress, would hurry home to change after her shift was over, and then head to the sleazy bars on the town's lower side. Sometimes she was accompanied by Minnie, but more frequently, by her latest boyfriend. She had a never-ending string of them.

Collette and Marcia met some of the men, those their mother dated for longer than a few weeks. One particular evening Marcia and Collette were playing a board game on the living room floor when Ray brought Julia home from work. He began to talk to the girls while Julia went to change. He seemed like a nice man and Marcia immediately liked him. She and Collette were laughing at a funny story he was telling when Julia returned. Her mother flushed and shot Marcia a sharp glance. Julia and Ray left immediately.

What was that about? Marcia wondered.

"He seems nice, huh?" Collette interrupted her thoughts. "Maybe Mom will marry him and I'll have a dad."

"You have a dad."

"I want one who loves me," Collette responded simply.

The next morning at breakfast, Julia surveyed Marcia. "How tall are you?"

"I'm five ten. Why?"

"I was just thinking that for a tall girl, you have a nice figure."

"Mom, I have a great figure. What does being tall have to do with it?"

"I never thought tall girls were attractive."

"Mom, you're five eight." Marcia stared at her mother who avoided her gaze and continued to drink her coffee and smoke her cigarette.

"Hi everybody."

Minnie couldn't have entered the kitchen at a better time. Marcia rose to leave for work. As she walked to the bakery, she thought about two unsettling encounters she had experienced with her mother. She was beginning to have the unpleasant feeling that her mother considered her competition for men.

Why would she even consider dating any of the men her mother dated? This wasn't the first time the thought had entered her mind though. At the beginning of summer a ringing phone had awakened Marcia. She could hear voices and loud music. A man asked for Julia.

"She's not here."

"Do you know where she is?"

"No, I don't."

"Are you her roommate?"

"No, I'm her daughter."

"How old are you?"

"I'm twenty."

"Julia has a daughter THAT old? Say, would you like to go out with me?"

"No. I'd like to get back to sleep." Marcia promptly hung up the phone. She only told Julia that she had missed a phone call, but gave no details.

"You didn't even get his name?"

"Sorry, I was sleepy."

A few days later, Julia asked Marcia how long she'd be staying.

"I told you I'd be here eight weeks, remember? Is something bothering you?"

Julia's tone was vacant. "Oh no."

Still there was an unsettling quiet about Julia. It was as if she was having difficulty considering something that bothered her tremendously.

Even Minnie had noticed. "Are you sure you're okay?"

Julia nodded.

"Well there's a new band at the Sagebrush. Dancing to good ole country music and a few drinks should make what's ailin' ya a whole lot better."

Chapter *Sixteen*

It seemed to Marcia that she'd always had a difficult time talking with her mother. Julia's view of the world seemed shallow to Marcia and her approach to difficult situations was to ignore them. Her answers to the girls' requests for information involving the normal curiosities, experiences, and feelings of children and teens were childish or she did not answer them at all. Yet, she was a bright woman. She had an extensive vocabulary and loved to read, even if the bulk of it was trashy magazines and novels. Marcia recalled an incident that occurred when she was around eight.

Julia had one of her silent spells which lasted an entire week. She said very little to the girls and nothing to Louis. Father was upset too. He was grumpy most of the time he was at home. But evidently Julia had something to say to someone. She was on the phone every time they returned from play.

"Who you talk'n to?" Marcia asked.

"Just friends."

One morning after Louis left for work, Julia hurriedly packed the suitcase and large shopping bag.

"Come on girls. The cab's here."

"Where are we going? Lee Ann asked anxiously.

"Uncle Peter and Aunt Alice said we could come for a Fourth of July visit on their ranch. What do you think of that?"

An air of excitement swept over the girls.

"Is this like a vacation? We've never been on vacation," said Lee Ann as Julia put everyone in the cab.

"Yes, it's a vacation all right," she said grimly.

They boarded the Greyhound at the bus station. It was exciting to be on a bus. Three new things in one day. The ranch would be the best part. They had never been on the ranch, and barely remembered their aunt and uncle, but Lee Ann and Marcia did remember their cousins Ingrid and Edna.

The cousins had come for a family gathering at Uncle Wilber's and were so wild and loud that Aunt Vivian finally had enough of them tearing through her house, slamming the doors, and hollering at the top of their lungs. She told everybody to settle down or she would take the belt to all of them, which seemed really unfair, as Edna and Ingrid were the only ones yelling and running through the house. The rest of the cousins thought it quite prudent to monitor Ingrid and Edna very closely after that and they made sure the pair stayed out of Aunt Vivian's sight.

It seemed to take forever for the bus to reach Chugwater. Uncle Peter was waiting for them when they arrived. He tipped his Stetson to Julia and lifted the suitcase, Marcia, and Lee Ann on to a filthy blanket in the bed of a very over-worked pickup. Julia took the bag of clothes and Collette up front. The scorching sun beat down on the brown and nearly barren land.

"You'll need to hang on tight as the road gets bumpy once we leave the highway. Use the blanket to grab hold of the sides; else you'll burn your hands." Uncle Peter arranged the blanket over the sides.

"Don't want you fallin' out." He made a little cough and spit a large amount of brown slime from his mouth before climbing into the cab. Lee Ann wrinkled her nose and grimaced at her sister.

"He chews tobacco," Marcia explained.

Bumping around like popcorn in the skillet was not the worst part of riding in the back. Clouds of dust enveloped the girls and they were frequently the target of ricocheting pebbles. Their hair whipped in every direction. Marcia was grateful for her shorter cut. Lee Ann was going to suffer when mom brushed out her long hair later that night. Still, it was fun to be driving down a country road with the wind swirling about them and the feeling of freedom offered by the wide open vistas.

As soon as the truck stopped, Edna and Ingrid jumped in.

"What are you wearing that for?" asked Edna, pointing at the pastel shorts and matching lace-trimmed halters Marcia and Lee Ann were wearing.

"Where's your jeans?"

"Mom wants us to wear these outfits."

"I think your boots will look funny with that."

"We don't have boots."

"You're going to wear those sandals in the barn and chicken coop?" asked Ingrid incredulously.

Ingrid and Edna were as ready to show them the barns and livestock as they were to see them; so as soon as they had a drink and washed their dust covered faces in the kitchen sink, they started out.

Lee Ann was enthralled. She petted the soft muzzles of the colts and calves. Marcia watched the cattle in the corral.

"When do you milk them?" she asked Edna.

"Milk 'em? Those are steers. We're going to sell 'em." Edna howled. "Hey Ingrid, Marcia thinks the steers are cows!" Both girls were now laughing. Marcia didn't think it was that funny.

"Do you want to see our bull?"

As they started toward another enclosure, Marcia stepped in something warm and soft. She was disgusted to see her foot was in the middle of a very large cow pie. The warm dung oozed over her toes. She began to cry. Her new sandals were ruined. She ran to find her mother.

Aunt Alice didn't seem too bothered that she had tracked into the house, but mother quickly sent her to the yard.

"Go over to the pump and wash off your foot."

"Don't worry," Aunt Alice called after her, "a little bull shit never killed anyone."

Marcia spent what was left of the afternoon on the porch letting her shoes dry and wishing for a pair of boots. She wasn't there long. Aunt Alice came out and rang the supper bell. Edna, Ingrid, and Lee Ann came round the east side of the barn toward the house.

Aunt Alice frowned.

Mother had Marcia and her sisters wash their hands at the kitchen sink. Then they sat down. Aunt Alice brought a large iron skillet full of fried potatoes to the table. The moment she set the skillet on the table, a long head of ashes dropped from her cigarette into the pan. Marcia looked at her mother. Julia flashed a warning look.

Guess I'll just pretend it's pepper, Marcia thought.

After everyone was served, Uncle Peter asked the visitors what they thought of the ranch. Lee Ann started by saying how wonderful the animals were, although she thought the bull looked awfully big and mean.

Uncle Peter laid his knife and fork down very slowly. "Did you girls go into the bull's pasture?"

Edna and Ingrid looked at their plates.

"Well, did you?"

"We weren't there very long," Ingrid said.

"And besides, he was on the opposite side of pasture," explained Edna.

"I've told you that animal is very dangerous. You've been told to stay out of there. Someone could have been hurt or killed. Both of you will go to bed early tonight."

Their cousins started to protest and complain about the severity of the punishment. Marcia couldn't believe how easily they had gotten off. She would have been spanked, sent to bed early for at least a week, and probably confined to the house. She'd take their punishment any time.

The thought had barely been formulated when Julia said, "Lee Ann and Marcia can go to bed early too."

"Mom..." Marcia tried to argue about the unfairness of being punished when they had done nothing wrong, but Julia was firm.

"It won't hurt you to go to bed early. You've had a long day."

Marcia couldn't believe it. Now they were again suffering because Edna and Ingrid couldn't behave.

Marcia joined Edna in her bedroom under the sloped attic roof. They were sharing Edna's double bed. Marcia was very aware that Aunt Alice was a terrible housekeeper when they first entered the house. Mother, who was always so clean, must have really wanted a vacation to stay at such a dirty place. The gray sheets looked like they had never been washed. The dust made swirls in the sunlight when she moved the covers. Dust coated the chest of drawers and night stand. She climbed in gingerly and she and Edna propped themselves on their elbows and tried to watch the sunset. The windows were so grimy and the piles of dead moths between the window and the screen so deep, that it was very difficult to see anything but a hazy light.

They stayed four days in all. Edna and Ingrid played as many tricks as they could think of on their unsuspecting cousins. Nothing to endanger their lives, just enough to get them scratched, bruised, or itchy, and their clothes torn.

Marcia was glad to get back to a clean house with indoor plumbing, but homecoming wasn't particularly pleasant. Julia had left a short note telling Louis that she was leaving with the girls for awhile. She said she'd stay with family, but didn't tell him where. His initial rage was spent by the time they came back and he welcomed them home with reserved irritation.

Chapter *Seventeen*

Marcia followed her plan for the unexpected windfall. She had paid cash for her contacts, purchased a few clothes, and deposited the princely sum of seventy five dollars into her savings account. She exited the bank with a great feeling of satisfaction. Even with so many expenditures,Marcia still had over a hundred dollars. She was feeling very secure. Her father had instilled in her at an early age the need to save, even in first grade...

Mrs. Cooper explained the savings stamp program. The children who participated would receive a booklet in which to paste their stamps. The stamps, which would be sold on Thursdays, would cost ten cents apiece. The books were stored in the bottom drawer of Mrs. Cooper's desk. Every Thursday, the books would be handed out so those purchasing stamps could add them to their books. When a book was full it would be sent home with the student. The child and a parent could take the book to the bank and receive a savings bond. The government would pay money on the bond and it would double in time. Marcia was amazed that a piece of paper could grow money and would be good for the country at the same time. That night she excitedly gave her father the permission sheet and the papers explaining the program. He studied her face.

"We won't be able to do it every week, maybe twice a month. How's that?"

"I get to do it?" Marcia broke into a big smile.

"Twice a month. Perhaps you can find a few bottles to redeem for extra stamps."

Marcia hugged her father.

Lee Ann began to cry, "I want to buy stamps too."

Before father could speak, Marcia said importantly, "Kindergarteners aren't allowed to do it. You have to be in first grade like me."

The years at Park School were busy, happy years. Marcia was a very good student and it was her grades that opened doors to another class of friends. Although she lacked many social graces and had a tendency to talk loudly, she had a zany sense of humor, and the enthusiasm, energy and imagination required for work on school projects and activities. She appeared open and self confident, but inwardly was plagued with doubts of her own worth and abilities, and as she matured she was driven to severe self criticism. She had a need to always be on the winning side and found it difficult to admit publicly or privately that her ideas might be wrong.

She and Lee Ann each had their own set of friends and usually didn't see each other on the playground. The exceptions were the times Lee Ann needed protection from a spiteful classmate. Although they frequently fought between themselves, Marcia never ignored her pleas for help and came to her assistance whenever Lee Ann asked.

Marcia seemed to be able to win privileges from their father, so Lee Ann went to her when she wanted some of the freedom Marcia enjoyed. She got to accompany Marcia to Wednesday night square dancing at the VFW hall and to the roller skating rink two miles from the house. As long as they were together father let them ride their bikes almost everywhere. He finally had a car and he would drive them to activities in the winter if his evening was free.

Marcia babysat for neighborhood families, did odd jobs for older neighbors, and continued to collect pop bottles. Father was very strict about saving the money she earned, yet she always seemed to have a bit of change in her pockets. It was not unusual for Marcia and Lee Ann to go to the movies together.

"Did mom give you the money? I thought she said she needed to save for the Kelvinator and couldn't give us anything right now."

"No, I saved some. I'll be glad when that refrigerator gets here and I won't have to empty that damn pan all the time. Don't understand why dad is such a tightwad. It wouldn't hurt for us to have some new things. Glad we have a bathroom. If dad had to pay for a tub and a toilet, we'd still have an outhouse and have to wash up in the sink." Lee Ann giggled.

They settled themselves and their popcorn before the movie started. Neither took much notice of the pudgy young man who sat next to Lee Ann. They were busy chatting and excitedly anticipating the start of the movie. Shortly after the start of the newsreel, Marcia felt Lee Ann stiffen. She turned to look at her sister. Even in the dimly lit theater, Marcia could see the shock on Lee Ann's face and the man's hand under her skirt and well up her thigh.

Marcia let out an explosion of expletives and said loudly, "You get your damn hands off my sister."

The man rose and hastily left the theater.

"You alright?"

"Yes."

They returned their attention to the movie. When they were walking home, Marcia said, "I don't think we should tell anybody about this. If dad found out, we'd never again be allowed out of the house." Lee Ann nodded in agreement.

Fighting was a constant at home. Mother called father "a stingy tightwad" and father called her a "spendthrift". The rest of the names were unrepeatable in the public square. Each accused the other of "running around". The girls could frequently hear screaming and dishes breaking. Marcia and Lee Ann escaped on their bikes in the summer, and in the winter, took refuge in the basement with Collette. Sometimes they would bundle up and go outside regardless of the cold. They would pretend they were skating and slide up and down the frozen sheet of ice created by the dripping water towers. Marcia would pull her sisters up and down Midwest Street on their rickety sled, or they would have snowball fights, or make snow angels.

It was early spring when their mother moved to a hotel. Their parents were again divorcing. This time, mother would be getting custody of the girls. Since she had no place to take them, insisting she could not support them on the sixty-six cents an hour wage she earned as a waitress, they would continue to live with their father. Julia would come every morning to get them ready for school and stay with Collette until it was time for her to go to work. Collette would then go to Mrs. Good's. Marcia would pick up Collette after school. She was in charge of her sisters and responsible for getting supper ready each evening. Father was home much less often. He was involved in the unions at the refinery where he now worked and was dating Velma.

Mother was now no longer there in the evenings either. This meant Marcia had the complete responsibility for the care of her siblings. She was poorly prepared for the shift of responsibility and power. When she couldn't achieve her wishes by commanding, she turned to meanness and bullying, tactics she'd learned well at the state-run orphanage and had observed to a lesser degree in her own home. Even though they needed and relied on her, her sisters began to fear and hate her.

One morning before school, Marcia approached her mother. "Why can't you take us? Sally said dad would have to give you child support."

"It won't be enough."

"Mrs. Boland does it on a waitress' salary and she had four kids."

"Well, I can't." Julia abruptly changed the subject. "I went to church with Allen."

"Who's Allen?"

"He's a man I met. Anyway, I went to church with him. It was very interesting. I think you would find it so."

"Find church interesting? What Church?"

"St. Anthony's."

"You can't mean the Catholic Church!" exclaimed 11 year-old Marcia.

"Everyone's heard those stories about what goes on in the convents and seminaries."

"The service seemed interesting."

"Mom, they worship statues. They're the most superstitious bunch of people you ever want to meet. And the pope controls all their thoughts."

"Well I still think you might find it interesting."

"Well I don't think so."

The route home from school took Marcia along the backside of the church's property. She had ignored it for years. Why had her mother even bothered to mention it? Now she was aware of the structure every time she passed it. Several weeks elapsed. One afternoon she had to wait after class to ask her fifth grade teacher a question about a report she had assigned.

Marcia told Lee Ann to go on ahead and pick Collette up. She would be as quick as she could. There were four classmates ahead of her. Why couldn't one of the others have had the same question she had ?

The playground was nearly deserted when Marcia left the building. As she started on her familiar route, she thought, *I can visit today. I'll just step inside and see what mom finds so damn interesting. All of my friends are gone. No one will see me go in there.*

By the way she surveyed the surroundings, one would have thought she was sneaking up on a disreputable enemy and, in truth, she believed she was. Her friends would have been horrified if they found out that she'd set foot in a Catholic church.

She scurried up the stairs and opened the door a crack. Why was the door so heavy? No sounds greeted her, so she strained to make an opening large enough for her to squeeze through and backed into the empty church. She turned slowly, still concerned that someone might be in the building. The afternoon sun streaming through the stained glass windows made them brilliant jewels and sent shafts of colored light on the empty pews.

Suddenly Marcia felt an overwhelming presence. Her heart quickened. Someone was here, the presence was almost palpable. Where? She quickly searched the church. A flickering red light caught her eyes and drew them to a softly glowing white marble altar in the front of the church. A small turret like structure with a gold door sat in the middle of the altar. She stared at it for some time and then she knew. Somehow God was present here. An overwhelming sense of awe filled her soul. She knew that she would become a Catholic and remain so for the rest of her life.

As she ran down the steps and started toward home, she was filled with a mixture of joy and peace. How could this have happened? She knew her decision would not be welcome news to her father, who had long ago given up his practice of the Catholic faith. Her friends, all Protestants, would not welcome the news either. Yet she knew beyond all doubt that her conversion to Catholicism would come to pass. She'd discuss it with Lee Ann tonight.

Collette was playing in her "dollhouse", a corner of the living room behind the couch where she kept her dolls and buggy. Marcia and Lee Ann were washing the supper dishes when Marcia broached the subject of the Catholic Church.

"I visited St. Anthony's today."

"You did? Does dad know?"

"Not yet. I'm going to become a Catholic."

"You are?" said Lee Ann in amazement. She wondered why Marcia hadn't yelled at them so much that night. She must have been really thinking about it.

"I heard somewhere that they have lessons on becoming Catholic on Saturday mornings. Do you want to come with me? It will be fun. Besides, it will get you out of the house."

Lee Ann wasn't sure about the fun part, but as Marcia was so pleased with the idea, she agreed to come.

"Let's wait to tell dad."

"Why?"

"I want to talk to mom tomorrow morning. She can find out about the lessons. Then I'll tell dad."

Their father was definitely not pleased with the idea of catechism lessons, but Marcia persisted until he agreed; besides, mother had already given her permission.

"I won't be taking you to anything that's got to do with the Catholic Church. You'll be walking. And I'm not giving you any money for books. The church is plenty rich; they can supply them."

"We understand," Marcia said quietly. She concealed her excitement with great difficulty.

So they began catechism at St. Anthony's School with Sister Ann. She was gentle and patient. Sunday mornings, they walked to Mass. Marcia took any free magazines that were available at the back of the church and read them carefully.

Sally noticed that Marcia's use of profanity had sharply decreased. "So what's going on with you?"

"What do you mean?"

"You're not talking the same way and I'm not sure what it is, but you're acting different."

"Well, I thought I'd clean up my mouth."

"Why?"

"It seems to be the right thing to do. I'm becoming a Catholic."

"No you're not."

"Well...yes I am."

"Why would you want to do that?"

"I think it's the church that Christ founded and wants us to belong to."

"That's just what you're being taught."

"No, I went to the library and looked in the encyclopedias. They listed all the popes since St. Peter. He's the one Jesus founded his church on. The popes go on from him."

Sally thought for a moment. "Can I go to the library with you? We can look up stuff about the Catholics together."

Marcia nodded. No one would be surprised. She and Sally frequently visited the library. They would page through the latest magazines. Marcia would read fairy tales and stories about King Arthur's court. Sally would read Sue Barton because she said she was going to become a nurse, and both enjoyed the newest Nancy Drew book. If they weren't in the mood to read, they could always peer through the stereoscopic viewers.

Marcia shared the magazines and the Baltimore Catechism with her friend. Sally asked Marcia if she could join them on Saturday mornings. She would get her mother's permission. They could become Catholics together. She would ask that very evening.

Sally didn't appear the next day, or the next. Marcia wondered if she was ill. On the third day of Sally's absence, Marcia went to her house. Her friend greeted her when she knocked at the door.

"Are you Okay?" Sally nodded.

"Can you come out?"

Sally shook her head. "Not until next week."

"Why? What happened?"

"I'll tell you later."

The week had ended and her friend was back. She had had quite an argument with her mother about joining the Catholic Church. Mrs. Boland made it abundantly clear to Sally that she was not becoming a Catholic and that she was never to mention the Catholic Church again. She and Marcia would be allowed to spend time together, but Marcia was prohibited from sharing her budding faith with Sally, and if the Catholic Church was part of their conversation again, she would not be seeing Marcia Gardinier at all.

Lee Ann and Marcia had completed their Saturday sessions and could say the basic prayers. They were prepared to be baptized. Louis was reluctant to consent. He put off the decision for several weeks. Lee Ann and Marcia continued attending Sunday Mass at St. Anthony's. One day when they returned home from Mass, he was waiting.

"I won't have one Catholic child. If your sisters want to be baptized and the priest will allow it, I'll consent." He fixed his gaze on Lee Ann. "Do you want to become a Catholic too?"

Marcia was more surprised than her father that Lee Ann didn't hesitate, "Yes, I do."

Before he could ask, Collette smiled and said, "Me too," in her childish voice.

Louis' last stipulation was met. Father MacCormack agreed to baptize all three girls.

So it was decided. A very disgruntled Louis would ask some friends of his to be godparents. They had known Louis and Julia years ago, when they were dating and when Louis still considered himself a Catholic.

The chosen time arrived, a gray and sleety day in March. Mother came with the Morans. This was to be the only time the girls would ever see their Godparents. It was amazing to Marcia that a ceremony of such consequence took so little time. It was arranged that Julia would begin attending Sunday Mass with the three of them. She would meet the girls at St. Anthony's. Collette was pleased that she could go with her sisters.

Sister Ann told Marcia and Lee Ann that she would need a few additional weeks to prepare them for their First Communions. As soon as she told them they could receive, the girls picked the earliest time; a daily Mass which started at eight. They could go to Mass and Communion and wouldn't be too late for class at Park School.

Marcia wanted to attend St. Anthony's for seventh grade, and to her surprise, she and Lee Ann would be allowed to go. Mother would buy the uniforms and father would pay the tuition.

She found her classmates to be very friendly and easily made new friends. She joined the choir, learned Latin, and sang for the funeral masses. The "Dias Irae" always filled her with dread at the thought of dying and facing judgment, yet something in the chant also appealed to her.

As usual, Marcia found relief at school. Open warfare had broken out at home.

One morning, before they left for school, Marcia noticed her mother folding the clothes she kept at the house.

"Why are you folding all your clothes?"

"I'm going to be picking them up tonight after work."

"How will you change for work if you take all your clothes?"

"I'm not going to be coming here anymore."

"You're not? So are you taking us tonight?"

Julia hesitated, "I'm coming with the police to get what's mine. We'll go then. Just don't tell your father."

Marcia was relieved. She was concerned that her father was going to marry Velma. She loved her father, but she knew that she and her sisters would fare very poorly if they had to live with him, Velma, and her two daughters. She felt they would be worse off than Cinderella. Their new faith would not be allowed, or if it was, it would be a constant source of friction.

She could eat little that night. The knock on the door came when Louis was getting Collette ready for bed. At first he was going to refuse Julia entrance, but he relented, given the presence of the policemen.

Marcia watched her mother collect the bags and some household goods she had purchased with her wages. Louis stood by mutely. Soon it would be time for Julia to tell them to get their things. Julia avoided looking at Marcia. One of the officers carried her bags to the waiting squad car. *Any time now*, Marcia thought, *mother would tell Louis they were all leaving*.

"Did you get everything, Ma'am?" the officer standing closest to Marcia asked Julia.

Julia scanned the room. "Yes I think so." She turned to go. Their mother was leaving them. There was a desperate, sinking feeling in the pit of Marcia's stomach. Julia had lied. She had never planned on taking her daughters. She was going to leave them...again. Marcia gently grasped the policeman's sleeve.

"Please sir, we don't want to stay here either," she said quietly.

She did not look at either parent during the ensuing whirlwind of activity. In a short time, the girls and a change of clothes were bundled into a police car and on their way to a foster home.

Mrs. Edwards, the social worker, visited the next morning. She talked with each girl separately and as a group. Marcia requested they be sent to a Catholic orphanage, if there was one. The social worker told her that there was St. Joseph's in Torrington. She would talk with their parents and would see the girls in a few days.

The foster home was not the place of refuge Marcia expected. The woman in whose home they were placed was elderly. Her fourteen-year-old grandson was a frequent visitor there and she had no control over him. He frequently hit and terrorized the younger girls, but hesitated to bother Marcia. Possibly it was because she threatened to flatten him and report him to the authorities.

One afternoon, he grabbed Collette's teddy bear from her and began to punch it. The nose, which was made of hard plastic, split from the assault. Collette shrieked in horror and began to sob. Marcia, who had been in another room, came flying through the door.

"What do you think you're doing? You big bully! You and your grandmother are going to be in so much trouble! Just you wait until Mrs. Edwards gets here!"

"You leave grandma out of this."

"She lets you push us around. No more! I'm reporting you both!" Marcia's face was contorted in anger and her fists were doubled up by her sides. No hurricane could have howled louder. She advanced on James.

Mrs. Jaynes hurried into the room. Marcia was ready for her.

"You're being paid to keep us here. Why is he allowed to bother us?" She grabbed Collette's bear and shoved it into the elderly woman's face.

"Look at this! See what he did to my sister's bear!" Mrs. Jaynes wrung her hands.

"I'm sure Jimmy didn't mean..."

"Oh yes, Jimmy did. He's nothing but a rotten brat and you allow him to bully us. I'm telling Mrs. Edwards when she comes."

Mrs. Jaynes was shaking. Foster care was needed income for her. She didn't want to lose it.

"Jimmy, you be a nice boy and go home." Mrs. Jaynes pushed her grandson towards the door.

"You need to get my sister a new bear."

Mrs. Jaynes shook her head, "I think this was just an accident," she said feebly.

"It was no accident. Neither are the bruises on my sisters' arms. We'll see what Mrs. Edwards thinks."

Mrs. Edwards came that afternoon. They were to stay with Mrs. Jaynes for the remainder of the week, and then they were going to Torrington. She didn't comment when Marcia related what had been happening at Mrs. Jaynes and showed her the bear and the bruises on Lee Ann and Collette, but Marcia heard her talking to Mrs. Jaynes and it seemed that she would no longer be eligible to do foster care. They didn't see her dear Jimmy again.

Chapter *Eighteen*

It seemed strange to Marcia that their father was the one taking them to St. Joseph's. He had neatly placed the clothes that had been left at the house on Midwest Street in the trunk of the car. There was plenty of room for the few things they had brought to Mrs. Jaynes. Marcia noticed a cardboard box in the corner of the trunk. Since her father had gone back into the house to check for any missed items, she decided to look at the contents of the box. It contained only shoes. She realized that most of their personal items were missing; no Nancy Drew books, her Hummel figurines, Lee Ann's miniature horses, Collette's toys.

She did not try to persuade herself that these might come later. She felt a dull ache in her chest as she mourned for not just those few possessions, but for all she and her sisters had lost. She would not tell Lee Ann and Collette what she knew; they would learn soon enough.

It was quite warm for April. The sun shone brightly and the ever present breeze was particularly soothing. Father said they could have the windows down. Collette sat between Lee Ann and Marcia. She busied herself singing lullabies to her doll. Lee Ann and Marcia looked out the windows.

Marcia felt a vast relief that she would no longer be refereeing her parents' fights, no longer be listening to their bitter accusations and learning of some of her parents' worst flaws, no longer being asked to choose sides.

She felt relief for no longer being responsible for trying to shield her sisters from some of the ugliness around them as their family disintegrated; and for no longer being responsible for their care every evening. She felt relief that they were out of foster care with that wretched Mrs. Jaynes, but she also felt guilty that her decision had helped put them in foster care in the first place.

Slowly Casper Mountain disappeared and the country gave way to rolling plains. Father occasionally pointed out some landmark, but he said little. The ride would have normally taken two-and-a-half to three hours, but father seemed to be in no hurry as they wended down I25. They stopped for lunch in Wheatland.

"It's a bit out of the way, but we can cut across and pick up 26 at Lingle and then go down to Torrington. You girls don't mind that do you?"

They didn't mind in the least.

The trip from Lingle seemed incredibly short. Suddenly they had arrived. A four-story yellow brick building rose from what looked like the middle of a farm. Tilled fields on the left vanished behind the building. A large barn and barnyard sat comfortably in front of the fields on the right.

Father rang the doorbell. It was seconds before a pleasant faced sister answered. She ushered them into a spacious marble-floored hall.

"You must be the Gardiniers. We've been expecting you. I'm Sister Marie Jude. Sister Angela has the older girls. She's at dinner now, but I'll help you until she's free. You can help the girls bring their things to their dorms, Mr. Gardinier."

Marcia and Lee Ann immediately recognized the arrangement. Two rooms, separated by the storage closet, with simple beds along opposite walls. Collette was assigned a bed in the closest room and told that she should leave her doll on her bed. Marcia and Lee Ann were assigned their beds in the other dorm and their clothes went to the storage room for marking.

"As you might notice, Mr. Gardiner, the closet is quite full. The townspeople are very generous to our children, and we get some of the best hand-me-downs." Sister proudly gestured to the full racks.

Marcia had little time to evaluate the clothes, but she was not impressed by most of what she saw. As poor as they were, mother had always made sure they were dressed well.

"The children are in the dining room for dinner. I'm sure your girls are hungry. If you'd like to say goodbye, I'll take them down."

Louis hugged and kissed each of them. "I'll come and visit as soon as I can."

They all descended to the first floor. Louis turned toward the entrance hall and the girls, guided by sister, headed to the dining room. Only one other person was in the long corridor. A very old sister bent with the weight of many years was slowly coming toward them. The thin skin of her round face was incredibly wrinkled. She looked so fragile that Marcia was sure the Wyoming wind could blow her away. They stopped directly in front of her.

"Mother Henrika, these are the Gardiniers; Marcia, Lee Ann, and Collette. They have just arrived from Casper." Mother grasped each girls hand and welcomed them warmly. Marcia was surprised by the firm, gentle grip. The face had a slight rosiness to the round cheeks, and twinkling black eyes looked straight into hers.

"Does your community have its motherhouse in Illinois?" Marcia asked her.

"No, we're in Milwaukee. Why do you ask?"

"I've been corresponding with a group of Third Order Franciscans who have a habit just like yours. I thought you might be the same order."

"No, my dear, we are not. There are many third orders and I believe several of us have similar habits. Ah, we can discuss that another time. I'm sure you are hungry. Sister will make certain you get something to eat. It is a pleasure meeting you."

As they resumed their walk, Sister Marie Jude looked at Marcia.

"Are you interested in religious life?"

"I was considering the Aspirancy."

"We have one also. The aspirants study at St. Mary's High School which is on the motherhouse grounds. It's quite beautiful there. Very green; not that Wyoming doesn't have a beauty of it's own. It's just not green. Well, here we are."

They paraded into the dining room. Twelve pair of eyes watched them intently. Sister introduced them and took Collette to a table with several younger girls. Marcia and Lee Ann found room at a table with five girls around their age. A short thin girl with curly hair and glasses left her nearly empty plate and retrieved plates, tableware, and napkins from the built-in cabinets by the dining room door.

"Where are you from?" she asked as she put the plates before them.

"We're from Casper," Lee Ann replied as she spooned a small amount of stew onto her plate. Both girls took the homemade bread and covered it thickly with butter. It was delicious.

The remainder of the meal was spent answering questions. They found that they were not the only ones here with at least one living parent. Some of the girls were true orphans, but many were here because one parent had died.

"My brother and I came to this stinkin' place when my mother died. We have to stay until we're eighteen, or graduate from high school, or my father remarries and takes us home. They're supposed to help us find jobs and a place to live when we're ready to leave. I can hardly wait to get out of this place. I'm sick of nuns telling me what I should and shouldn't do. I'd leave next year when I turn sixteen, but my dad won't allow it."

The speaker was a bony girl with small squinty eyes, a large nose, and a wild mess of black hair. She made no effort to keep her voice down and Marcia noticed that the younger children cast fearful glances her way.

"Aren't you grateful for the help the sisters are giving you?" Marcia asked.

The other girl glared at her.

"You wait until you're here awhile and see if you like it." Her voice was shrill.

"I'll have to do that. So far, it seems pretty decent."

The girl stood so quickly that she tipped her chair over. It clattered as it hit the floor. Her fists were clenched by her side.

"Are you calling me a liar?" The room was suddenly very quiet. Marcia looked steadily at her as she appraised her from across the table. Her first thought was that Gertrude was even taller than she was. Her second thought was that Gertrude would make a very frightening witch on Halloween. Gertrude hadn't moved, but remained towering over the table.

"What I was saying was that I have a different opinion than you do, and we're all entitled to our opinions. Don't you agree?" Marcia had deliberately made her voice very soft.

She had just finished speaking when Sister Angela returned. Gertrude glared at Marcia, "I don't like you. You had better stay out of my way." She jerked her chair into its normal position and swept past sister and into the hall.

Sister Jude Marie was close behind Sister Angela. She introduced the girls.

"You can help the others clean up. I'll assign chores for you tomorrow."

"Would there be a place for me in the kitchen? I really like to cook." Marcia looked hopeful.

Sister Angela thought for a minute. "I was thinking you could help with the younger children. But if you want the kitchen, why don't you introduce yourself to Sister Dominic and see if she can use you? Turn left as you go out the door."

Marcia left immediately. She didn't want Sister Angela changing her mind and assigning her to care for the younger children. She had had enough of that.

Sister Dominic was a tall sturdy woman with a creamy complexion. The color of her normally rosy cheeks was heightened by the heat from the stove. She was wiping steam from her glasses as Marcia entered. She seemed younger than any of the sisters Marcia had met so far.

"Sister Dominic?"

"Yes."

"I'm Marcia Gardinier. My sisters and I arrived today. Sister Angela sent me to see if you need any help in the kitchen."

"The work is hard and you'd be here every day. This place gets very hot in the summer."

"I think I can manage. I like to cook."

"It would be more like scrubbing pots and pans and serving than cooking."

"That's okay too. Can you use me?"

"My usual help, Mrs. Dixon, had to go to her sister's to help with a new baby. Why don't you come right after Mass tomorrow? Right now, it's time for Night Prayer. You'd better get to chapel."

"Oh, thank you very much. Chapel's on the first floor?" Sister nodded and Marcia was off.

All in all, it had been a good day. This place seemed much better than the state orphanage in Casper, all except for Gertrude. The nuns seemed nice. She had seen Lee Ann and Collette during recreation after night prayer. She hoped that the rest of the school year would be good. Perhaps mother would find a way to take them home when summer came and she could return to St. Anthony's.

It seemed so different to be sleeping in a bed by herself again. She and Lee Ann had shared the double bed since they had moved to Midwest Street.

The decision to work in the kitchen was a sound one. Marcia did do pots and pans, but she also helped prepare meals and served in the priest's dining room. She loved Sister Dominic and spent most of her free moments working alongside her and happily talking about her plans, school, whatever interested her at the moment. When summer came, Sister would send her to the pool for at least part of the afternoon so Marcia could have free time and exercise, and probably for Sister to give her overworked ears a much-needed rest.

Marcia was not a good swimmer and did not like the water in her nose and eyes, but she did try to swim and enjoyed watching her sisters having fun. She had made no close friends at the orphanage. She had started to form a friendship with the girl who helped them on the first night, but she left to go to live with her aunt about two months after Marcia arrived.

Gertrude had developed a blind hatred for Marcia and she influenced the three remaining older girls against her. For her part, Marcia thought they were the stupidest bunch she had ever seen and would talk down to them, or bring up topics she knew they didn't understand, or had never heard about. She also felt that Gertrude was mentally ill and could be dangerous. She wondered why the sisters let her stay there and she ignored her as much as possible.

Gertrude liked to pick on the younger girls. Her favorite place to trap them was the bathroom. More than once, Marcia came to her sisters' aid and often stepped in to challenge Gertrude when she was after the littlest girls. Although Gertrude was taller, and probably stronger than Marcia, she backed off when challenged.

One day Marcia heard Gertrude and her cronies planning to attack her as she passed the basement cloak room on her way to the kitchen. She avoided the basement from then on unless everyone was getting coats or other outdoor wear and got Sister Dominic's permission to use the first floor corridor on her way to chores.

Marcia did have several friends at the junior high and looked forward to the time at school. As usual, she was an excellent student and received recognition for projects she and her classmates had produced. This, and the fact that Marcia was spending so much time with the sisters firmly cemented the wedge between her and the others.

The tension came to a head one night when Marcia was washing the china in the butler's pantry adjacent to the priest's dining room. She had been so absorbed in her work and singing so loudly, that the sharp rap on the pantry door startled her. She opened the door to find Gertrude and three others clustered there. There were no smiling faces in the group and the hostility was tangible.

"Was that you singing?"

"Yes, why?"

"Is Sister in there?"

"No, she should be here in a bit." Marcia lied. Sister was busy in the kitchen and that meant she was the length of the building away from the pantry and right now that was way too far away.

"What takes you so long in there?"

"Father had guests and it's taken a bit longer to clean up."

"Why are you so happy?"

"I didn't know it was a crime to be happy. Besides, I just heard that I've been accepted to enter the Aspirancy."

"The what?"

"I'll be entering the convent after eighth grade."

The atmosphere changed with lightening speed. Two of the girls looked at their feet, one cleared her throat, and Gertrude took a step back.

"Oh. We just thought we'd see where you were."

"Thanks for checking on me," Marcia said coolly.

Marcia and her sisters had no more trouble with Gertrude.

While St. Joseph's was a respite for Marcia, it was a poor substitute for home for Lee Ann and Collette. The girls had separate monthly visits with each parent. Each time they begged to come home, mother always insisted she could not afford it and father, who was now married to Velma, referred them back to their mother who had custody of them.

The visits were usually no longer than a day and consisted of going out to dinner. As father had a car, they had the additional pleasure of a drive in the surrounding country. Mother traveled by train. The station was close to the orphanage, so the girls were allowed to walk over to meet her and accompany her back when she left. They spent her visits walking the grounds or sitting in the parlor.

Lee Ann became more subdued as their second summer at St. Joseph was ending.

"Tell me again. How long will you be gone?"

"I'll be coming home next summer. We can't afford for me to come over any of the holidays. Mother should be able to get you two home before I come back," Marcia smiled brightly. Lee Ann just looked at her.

"Do you really have to go?"

"I do if I want to become a sister. My bus leaves at midnight tomorrow. I promise I'll come and kiss you goodbye. Don't be so sad. We'll see each other next summer and you and Collette will be home."

Chapter *Nineteen*

Marcia was not only leaving the state for the first time, she was traveling almost a thousand miles from home. The trip would take thirty- four hours. Excitement trumped nervousness and she spent most of the time gazing out the window marveling at each change in the passing countryside. The sack lunch Sister Dominic had packed for her would cover breakfast and lunch, then she would need to buy food when the bus made restaurant stops. Father Crandell and the sisters had given her ten dollars to cover her needs since mother said she had no money to spare after buying her several pair of the required shoes, and father told her he would never speak to her again if she entered the convent.

She found a taxi at the station and settled into the seat with a feeling of relief. She was almost there. She found the beautiful trees and the greenery of the Midwest gardens and lawns to be refreshing.

What a beautiful place this is. Thank you Lord for the gift of sight, she thought. The road to the motherhouse skirted Lake Michigan. Marcia was astounded at its size and beauty. She had never seen so much water. If this was a lake, what would an ocean look like?

She was one of the early arrivals. Over the next few days, forty teens would present themselves for formation. They were measured for school uniforms and the long black dress of the aspirancy. The dress had a stiff white celluloid collar. Each aspirant had two net veils, a black one for weekdays and a white one for Sundays. These were held in place by a bobby pin that matched the color of the veil.

All were assigned a cell in one of two large rooms. The cell consisted of a metal framed bed and nightstand which held each girl's underwear and nightgowns and an enamel basin used for sponge bathing. The nightstands had a towel rack on the side for towels. During the day the basin sat upside down on the stand covering a glass, a soap dish, and a toothbrush. Wash cloths were laid over the basins to dry. During the night, the basin sat full of water for the next morning's use. A private space was made by closing the curtains that hung on the frame attached to the head and foot of each bed. The frames must have been designed for shorter persons, because Marcia could see over the top.

The Mistress of Aspirants was Sister Mary Roseanne. She was tall, very thin, and quite pretty. She smiled often. She radiated a sense of contentment. Marcia would find that she also possessed an extreme amount of patience

There were a few odd girls in the class, but most were very normal teens from strongly Catholic two-parent homes. Because of her divorced parents and her chaotic background, she had needed special permission to enter. She was acutely aware that she was different from the others and she said little about her family life. The association with her fellow aspirants and the kind and dedicated sisters, would help Marcia continue on the path of healing which she had begun at St. Joseph's. They would help her develop more normal social behaviors and attitudes.

Within months, the girls with unusual behaviors were asked to leave. Marcia did not realize that Sister had initially considered her as well, but Marcia made rapid improvement in her demeanor and had adjusted well to life in the Aspirancy. Her interactions with the others were positive and she appeared to be well liked.

The structured days were full from five-thirty in the morning to the end of study hall at ten nightly. They had religion class before the full school day, and even before they arrived at that classroom, they had met for Morning Prayer, attended Mass, eaten breakfast, and done morning chores.

They returned to the convent for lunch. Marcia was delighted that it was one of the times they were allowed to talk. They had a reader for breakfast and dinner unless it was a special feast and Sister granted permission for them to talk at meals.

A generous after-school snack was offered. The girls could help themselves to left-over desserts, homemade bread and jam, sandwiches, fruit, sweet rolls, and unlimited whole milk which came from one of the convent farms. Marcia's attendance at snack was nearly perfect and her weight began to climb.

Unless it was raining heavily, snack was followed by a brisk walk to the shores of Lake Michigan or around the extensive, beautiful grounds. Usually they recited the rosary as they walked, but if they had finished praying and were still walking, Sister allowed them to talk. It was time for silence once they entered the motherhouse.

The limited time before dinner could be used for spiritual reading, a visit to the chapel, assigned chores, or to start studies.

Evening prayer was following by an hour of recreation which all were required to attend. With such structure it was incredible that some girls, usually Marcia and her friends, could find time to get into trouble. Penance for such behavior was generally extra prayer time. Sister Roseanne would specify the intention for the penance. Marcia was a frequent visitor to the chapel and prayed for a multitude of intentions.

Great silence followed recreation. It was a serious matter to be communicating in any manner with one another after the bell for silence rang. The term "custody of the eyes" was the phrase that covered all eye contact.

The lights in the dorm went off at nine, so most of the aspirants prepared for bed early and then returned to the study hall if they needed extra time for their lessons. Others retired at this time. Marcia was not one of the early preparers. She would try to finish her studies first and then hurry to the dorm to get ready for bed. Usually, she entered the room with only minutes before the lights went out. There was always a line to fill basins for the nightly ablutions and to empty and refill them for morning. This meant Marcia was usually fumbling in the dark.

"Why don't you get ready sooner?" asked Barbara whose cell was head-to-head with Marcia's.

"I don't know. I just get absorbed in what I'm doing."

"Well, I can hear you trying to get ready for bed."

"I'll try to get there sooner."

It was easier to say she would try, than to do it. A few days after their conversation, Marcia came scurrying in as usual. She hastily pulled her curtains and turned for her basin. Then she heard a stifled snicker and looked up to see her friend, who was equally tall, peering over the curtain.

Barbara's eyes were dancing. Marcia glanced down at her basin in time to see a big toothpaste smiley face on her washcloth. Then she was engulfed in darkness. She could hear Barbara laughing as she pulled her thoroughly knotted gown from her stand and finally located her toothbrush and glass under her pillow. She finished preparing for bed, pulled back the covers, and tried to lie down. Her feet would go nowhere. The bed had been short sheeted. The frame of Barbara's bed was shaking. Marcia gave a good natured sigh and started to remake her bed.

Marcia wondered if both of them should see Sister Roseanne for a penance. After all, they had broken great silence. They discussed it the next day and decided to let this one slide.

"Where did you learn to short sheet a bed?"

"My brothers were always doing it to someone. What did you think of those knots? Weren't they top notch?"

"They were something. I really had a hard time with the sleeves."

"I know. I could hear the struggle."

Both of them laughed.

Chapter *Twenty*

Sunday mornings, Sister had all three classes for formation. The freshmen were dismissed first, the sophomores second, and the juniors last. Those dismissed early would go to chapel or out to the grounds for spiritual reading and rosary. Marcia longed for the time her class would get to have more intense studies.

Although Marcia had told Julia that she was not free on Sunday mornings, Julia frequently disregarded this information and would call during this time. It was always some emergency that involved her sisters, now that they were home, and she was usually crying when she called.

Marcia's heart sank every time they were interrupted by the ringing phone in sister's office. Sister would excuse herself to answer and then beckon Marcia to the office and softly close the door behind her. It was always the same. Sometimes Marcia found Julia so irritating that she would become quite brusque and her voice would rise above her usual hushed tones. One of the worst calls was just before the summer home visit.

After her usual complaints, Julia whined, "This is so hard. Maybe I should just send them back to Torrington."

"Don't you dare! Don't you even think about it or I'll never speak to you again! Do you understand me? You're their parent. Act like it!" Marcia returned the receiver to its cradle much harder than she had intended.

When she exited the office, Sister had ended the lessons and they were forming teams for the softball game which would start after lunch. Right now they had an hour of free time.

"Marcia, could I see you in my office for a moment? Close the door, would you, and have a seat." Sister's voice was kind.

"Sister, I didn't mean to be so loud." Marcia sank into the chair opposite the desk. "It's just that she's threatening to send my sisters back to the orphanage."

"I can understand your frustration and it is admirable that you care for your sisters, but she is your mother and you owe her your respect." Sister looked at her kindly, "Can you understand that? God gave you the gift of life through her."

Marcia sat quietly for a minute and then she nodded.

"I want you to dedicate a rosary for your family today."

"I can do that."

"I also want you to send your mother a note of apology." Marcia nodded again.

"One last thing. You have not written to your father this month. You need to get that done today."

"Sister, he has never answered any of the letters I've sent this year."

"I know, but you must always try. He is your father. Two letters in my office this evening."

"Yes Sister."

"You may go now. I think you've been chosen as catcher. Just keep the glove up so you don't get hit in the face again."

"I'll try. Jean's got a really good arm and throws the ball hard."

They smiled at each other.

Chapter *Twenty-one*

Marcia was glad summer vacation was short. She would have preferred to spend the summer at one of the institutions the sisters staffed. She and her friend Lucy had done that for the shorter vacations and it had been a good experience for her. She stopped for a day to visit the sisters at St. Joseph's before going home.

"Home" was a small apartment in a dark basement that was prone to mold, especially the shower. Mother was frequently absent. She worked during the day and spent the evenings at the bars with her friends. Marcia tried to follow her prayer routine, but found little privacy or quiet time in the cramped quarters.

She mistakenly tried to assume her original role with her sisters, but they had been too long on their own and considered her to be a bossy intruder. The situation usually deteriorated into fighting that left Marcia feeling guilty and realizing that she had much to do if she was to effect permanent changes in her behavior. When this happened, her sisters united as one in their hate for her.

During the periods of reconciliation, the three did have times of simple games and the enjoyment of each other's company. Her sisters were grateful for the interventions with their mother; but all in all, the visit was not satisfactory to anyone.

Her father did not return her phone calls and after two weeks, she gave up trying to contact him. He was not involved with the younger girls either. Marcia understood from her sisters that he was quite busy with Velma's daughters.

The new school year was approaching. Marcia accompanied her sisters downtown to shop for school clothes. She helped them make choices within their meager budget. Careful scrutiny of the sales racks gave them a good start for the year.

Finally, it was time to leave.

"Do you really want to go back?" Julia asked her for what felt like the tenth time that week.

"Yes Mom, I really do."

"Well, I don't know how I'm going to manage."

"You should do fine. The girls are pretty self sufficient. I taught Lee Ann to grocery shop and both of them can fix simple meals."

"I don't know. I think they would be better off in Torrington."

"Let's not start that again. The girls are here and they need to stay here. Besides, you promised me that they could stay."

"It's just too much for me. If you would stay and help me..."

Marcia interrupted, "I'm going back and you are going to keep your promise."

Julia sighed.

Marcia boarded the train that evening for her second year of formation.

Chapter *Twenty-two*

Marcia easily fell back into the familiar routine of religious life. In retrospect, she would consider this her best year. She and her classmates were able to take the midnight hour in the perpetual adoration chapel. She loved the time of quiet prayer. Each day seemed to integrate her more firmly into convent life.

This was also her busiest year for finding trouble. Silence was a difficult discipline for Marcia and some of her friends, but they truly tried to follow the rule. Since they were not ever allowed to talk in the dorm, they had to find a way to contact each other when the needed friend was in their dorm room.

One particularly cold winter day found Marcia, Barbara, and several others huddled on one of the long screened porches the massive stone convent had on each of its five floors. These porches were used as sleeping quarters when the sisters came home for the summer, but in the winter these unheated areas provided sheltered storage for the metal frames and mattresses.

The group was gathered near a dorm window which Barbara was quietly tapping.

"Why don't you just go in and get Janet?" queried soft-spoken Margaret.

"Because we're not supposed to talk in there."

"I know that. Couldn't you just grab her sleeve and pull her out here?"

"That's just as bad as talking."

"Do you think pounding on a window is any better?"

Barbara's taps had become much harder since her first attempts to get Janet's attention had not worked.

Suddenly the curtains parted and Janet was raising the window.

"Come out here so we can talk."

Janet nodded and grabbed the window frame, placed her feet on the sill and started to swing through. The group watched in disbelief as her foot caught on a half-full five gallon container of holy water and knocked it out of its stand. It shattered and sent water and glass across the porch floor.

Marcia wanted to laugh. Janet's face was bright red. The others were frozen in place with a mixture of astonishment and horrified amusement on their faces.

"We'd better hurry and get this cleaned up," Marcia said as she stifled her laughter.

"Why didn't you just come through the door? It's so close." Asked Margaret.

"So, why didn't you just come to get me?"

Barbara had reached the cleaning bin and was tossing rags to everyone.

Jean had found a trash barrel and was throwing glass into it.

She cautioned them, "Don't throw the rags with glass in them into the wash bin. We'll just have to throw them away."

"My rag's starting to stick to the floor!" Judy exclaimed.

"I'll get a little hot water from the bathroom and we can pour it on your rag. Let me get my glass." Margaret left hurriedly.

Pouring more water on that which was freezing, proved to be useless.

"We've got most of the glass. What are we going to do about all this water?" Jean looked at her fellow culprits.

Judy spotted the rag-rug by the outside door. She grabbed it and threw it over the sheet of ice that was forming.

"Someone will trip over that," Margaret observed.

"Oh no they won't. See, the rug will be stuck to the floor in no time. I figure by the time spring comes, the water will have evaporated and the postulants won't have too much to clean up."

Judy's line of reasoning seemed perfect. Everyone nodded.

"Glad we're not postulants in the spring," Barbara whispered in Marcia's ear.

"So what was all this about anyway?" Janet asked.

"We wanted you to practice your lines for the play tonight and didn't want you to forget the script."

"You couldn't have told me that at dinner?"

"No, we have a reader tonight."

Just then the dinner bell rang.

"I'm the reader and I'm supposed to be there ahead of time," and with that, Jean hurried away.

Marcia and Lucy were now being invited to spend most of their vacations with classmates. This gave Marcia a chance to see other areas of Wisconsin and Illinois. She especially loved the countryside and the small farming communities.

Spring was fast approaching. It was already April 1st. They were well into Lent and the winter blahs were still hanging around. Marcia felt that a few good pranks would certainly lighten the atmosphere. She just needed to find a good set-up.

She didn't have long to wait. Her class had religion before school this particular day. They arrived to find an empty classroom. The usually punctual priest was nowhere to be found.

"Hey everybody, I have the perfect April Fool's joke for Father. Let's divide up and hide in the closets. When Father comes for class he'll find an empty room. When he gets up to his desk we can run out shouting "April Fool's."

Everyone except Margaret thought it was a great idea. "I don't think Sister will like it."

"You are such a wet blanket," chided Jean.

"Okay." said Marcia, "You stay out and tell Father that Sister kept all of us for a lecture. Tell him we'll be just a few minutes late. We'll jump out after you've said that."

Thirty girls crammed themselves into three small storage closets and waited. Several minutes elapsed before they heard Margaret's greeting to their instructor, then they exploded from the hot cramped closets yelling "April Fool's".

The kindly priest smiled and said, "I think that was a pretty good joke." He called the class to order.

Another opportunity for a prank presented itself right before dinner.

Marcia was working in the kitchen and was getting ready to start serving. She could hear Janet humming as she approached the dutch door which separated the kitchen from the refectory. The door had a large lazy susan which could be used as a pass through for dishes. Marcia wondered why Janet wasn't in the kitchen with her. What could possibly be delaying her? She must be daydreaming. Marcia could fix that!

She put her ill-conceived plan into effect immediately. Gripping the susan's edge, she gave it a robust turn and hollered, "April Fool's!"

A five gallon bucket of milk sent a churning white fountain into the air before drenching the tile floor; while the remains of a large glass bowl of pudding, saved from breakage by the heavy rag rug on which it landed, emptied itself of the sticky contents on the receiving rug.

"What are you doing?" Janet's eyes were wide with shock as she looked at the mess.

"I thought you were daydreaming and I was going to scare you," Marcia replied.

"I got here late and was cleaning up after snack."

Sister Lucinda, the cook, was rolling her eyes. "You'd best get that mess cleaned up. Dinner is ready to be served."

Marcia had just retrieved the bucket when the dinner bell sounded and Mother Superior entered the kitchen on her way to her dining room. Mother quietly surveyed the scene and walked on without a word. Marcia was very late for dinner that evening.

She was not surprised when Sister Roseanne beckoned her to the office that night, but she was surprised by the topic.

"What happened in the religion classroom today?"

"Not much that I can think of, just another good lesson."

"I was thinking about Father Lieblien."

"Ohhh. Do you mean my April Fool's joke?"

"Yes, that would be it. Would you like to explain?"

Marcia recounted the whole story and ended by observing that Father had thought it quite clever.

"Mother Superior was not of the same mind."

"Mother Superior! How could she have possibly found out about that?"

"Mother did hear of it and thinks that your behavior was very disrespectful to a priest. As a penance, I want you to go to the chapel and say a decade for Father and you are to publicly apologize to him at your next class."

"Yes, Sister."

"I did hear from Sister Lucinda that you were a bit busy today. Were you responsible for the mess in the kitchen and the delay in coming to the table?"

"Yes, Sister."

Marcia's explanation was interrupted by Sister.

"I'm quite aware of the details. I would suggest that you try for more decorum in your behavior and that you think about your impulses before putting them into action."

"Yes, Sister. What's my penance?"

"No penance. Go pray for Father. Remember to ask for the guidance of the Holy Spirit every morning."

Marcia did not see Sister shake her head and stifle a laugh after she had left.

Chapter *Twenty-three*

The summer vacation following Marcia's second year was slightly improved over the first year. Mother had moved to an apartment on the main floor of an old house which was much better than the dank basement. Lee Ann was now married and Collette was busy with her friends. The relationship between Marcia and Collette was more relaxed. Julia was still working during the day and out with friends at night. Marcia's attitude and feelings toward her mother could only be described as restrained politeness with measured respect.

As the end of summer approached, Marcia was not surprised to hear Julia suggesting that she could stay home and finish high school in Casper. Her answer never wavered.

"Mom, I'm going back. You're doing fine."

She was, however, surprised by a phone call from her father.

"I suppose that you'll be returning to Milwaukee in a few weeks."

"Yes, I am."

"Well, I just wanted to tell you that I have appreciated your letters. Velma and I were wondering if you'd like to come for dinner before you go back. We're not inviting anyone else. Just wanted to talk with you."

Marcia hesitated briefly.

"I guess I can do that. What day are you thinking about?"

On the appointed night, Marcia changed from street clothes into her black dress and waited tensely for Louis.

He came promptly at six. She was relieved that Collette was still at her friend's when she left.

The evening went surprisingly well. After their initial discomfort with her attire, her father and Velma relaxed and were full of questions about her life. They were impressed by the strong academic schedule, and quite interested in her daily routine and her description of the convent grounds.

Marcia felt she was dispelling some long held myths about religious life, but was not naïve enough to think she had banished prejudice against the Catholic faith.

When her father volunteered to take her to the depot for her return trip to Milwaukee, Marcia accepted. This would save her mother the expense of a cab.

Chapter *Twenty-four*

Jean was certainly excited about something. She had spotted Marcia coming up the walk with her suitcase and met her inside the entrance.

"Did you hear the news?"

"I just got here, silly girl. What news?"

"They've just added another year to the Aspirancy. We won't be postulants next year."

"Why?"

"Something to do with maturity and the drop out rate, I'm sure."

"Another year? Why does it have to start with our class?"

"We'll be divided into two groups. I think we get to keep Sister Roseanne."

"Well, I'm for that."

They lingered in the entrance for a few minutes so they could exchange news of their respective summers.

"I'd better get upstairs. Sit by me at dinner and we can talk. Sister always give us privileges our first night back."

"Before you go, I want to ask you something. Would you be interested in coming to my house for Christmas? I'm asking early before anyone else does."

"Are you kidding? I would love to."

They left the entrance and went quietly up the stairs.

Unpacking took very little time. Marcia went to the adoration chapel to thank the Lord for a safe journey and the graces necessary for the new year. She returned to the common room and joined in the exuberance of greeting old friends and the shock of learning about classmates that had dropped out. It was a time of relaxed enjoyment. School would start in two days.

The Christmas holidays seemed slow to arrive. Perhaps it was because school had been so intense that Marcia was unusually ready for a break.

Jean's large family was part of a family of farmers. As they drove through the snowy countryside, Jean looked at Marcia with trepidation. "I hope you won't mind the lack of plumbing."

"You don't have any plumbing?"

"We have water at the kitchen sink and a shower in the basement where the pasteurizer is, but you'll have to use the outhouse."

"Why are you telling me now?"

"I thought you might not want to come if you knew."

"Of course I'd come. We're friends aren't we? I'm just happy you thought to ask me."

They smiled at each other. Of all Marcia's friends, Jean was her favorite, even though they weren't supposed to have favorites.

Jean's siblings accepted Marcia instantly. The old farmhouse was spacious and had a warm, worn comfort to it. She loved being involved in the preparation for Christmas and the busyness a large family naturally generates. Jean's sisters closest in age were as spontaneous and as lively as Jean and Marcia. The full, happy days filled a hunger in Marcia of which she'd been unaware. She hurried through her rosary and daily prayers so she could rejoin the family downstairs.

It was a seemingly trivial occurrence that flipped Marcia's emotional life into turmoil.

Jean had six sisters and two very outnumbered brothers. The older was home from college for the holidays and was barely seen as he spent most of his time with his fiancée. This left David with the girls. He was about two years Jean's junior. He was quite tall, slender, easy going, and had a subtle sense of humor. He was also quite handsome. One afternoon David suggested they go sledding.

"We've been cooped up too long. Let's get outside."

"I didn't see any hills. Where do you sled?" Marcia was puzzled.

"We don't need hills. We attach the sled to the back of the tractor and go around the barnyard," explained Jean.

"Do you want to try it?"

"I'll give it a shot."

They all bundled up and headed for the barnyard. Marcia wanted to watch a few times before she committed herself to the sled.

"We've all gone. It's your turn," Jean was encouraging.

"C'mon 'fraidy cat," David called from the tractor.

"David, no stunts. She's not been on the sled before."

Jean's admonition was promptly ignored. Marcia had barely grasped the handles when the sled lurched forward. The fence posts whizzed past her in a dizzying circle.

Were they all going this fast? The tilt-a-whirl had nothing on this, Marcia thought to herself.

Suddenly there was a sharp jerk and Marcia went tumbling. She lost her grip on the sled. She hadn't even noticed the barbed wire post until it stopped her. David was the first one to reach her. He slipped an arm under her shoulders and started loosening her coat from its entanglement. "Are you okay?" His face was filled with concern.

Marcia started to laugh.

"I'm really fine. That was some ride."

David's face relaxed and he smiled at her.

Marcia had noticed David when she first arrived and initially was very reserved with him, but several times when he sat beside her as the family played board games or did a puzzle, she had been pleased. When he looked at her, there was something in those beautiful brown eyes.

Then Jean was kneeling in the snow beside her. David had finished freeing her coat and helped her into a sitting position, his arm still giving unneeded support to her back.

"I told you not to go so fast," Jean glared at her brother. "Are you okay?"

"I'm fine, really I am." Marcia felt anything but fine.

If the holidays had been slow in coming, they were exceedingly rapid in passing. David filled all of Marcia's thoughts and time; his presence was sweet. He continued to sit near her when the opportunity presented itself.

"What's the forecast for tomorrow?" Marcia asked as they gathered around the breakfast table. She was hoping for a blizzard which would buy them a bit more time at the farm.

"Clear and cold. You girls should have no problems traveling," Jean's father remarked as he passed around the oatmeal.

Marcia felt a stinging disappointment. She had never been reluctant to return to the convent before, but this had been the best Christmas she had ever had, not even considering David. Her only consolation was that she would see Jean's family when they came for a visit in the spring. She would not be coming back to the farm, as Sister only allowed one visit to any classmate's home. Perhaps someday...They left after breakfast the next morning.

Marcia tore into her studies. She also spent more time in the chapel as she wrestled with her thoughts. A sense of guilt lay heavily on her conscience and yet she sought no guidance from Sister Roseanne or her confessor.

"Marcia, can I see you in my office?"

Marcia sat in the familiar chair facing Sister.

"You seem to be losing weight. Are you feeling alright?"

"I'm fine."

"Something seems to be bothering you. Anything I can help you with?"

"No," Marcia lied. "I've just been busy with my studies." They sat in silence for a moment.

"You may go. Know that I'm always available for you."

"Thank you, Sister."

How could she tell Sister that she was thinking of leaving or the reason behind it? Had Marcia, who was so mature in many areas and so used to shouldering her burdens alone, been as mature emotionally, she would have been able to discuss her dilemma and find relief; but she could only wait and pray.

The spring visit was disappointing. How could it be otherwise? She could only glance at David. Did he notice that she had lost almost twenty pounds? She had hoped that somehow, regardless of the distance, something would come of this attachment.

She was home about a month at summer break, before she wrote to tell Sister she would not be returning. She had already found a part-time job at a bakery and had enrolled in school for her senior year. Julia was delighted as she now had someone to help manage the house and Collette.

Chapter *Twenty-five*

It seemed that the more things changed, the more some things stayed drearily the same.

Nurses training had not deterred Julia from continuing to expect Marcia's help over the summer. She always insisted she could not manage without her.

Marcia was certain she could get a summer job at the bakery. Now that she had the scholarship, there was to be no more wasted time pondering career decisions for her next two years. She was going to be a nurse and finish her training. Financially, she could take care of herself, so Julia would never have that burden again.

The summer passed quickly enough. Even her relationship with Collette was improved; most probably because each was busy with her own interests. Marcia saw Lee Ann only once in the eight weeks as their visits remained strained. She did visit with her father who was proud to hear that she was doing well, but never asked if she had any needs or offered any financial support.

She told Julia that she needed to return to school a week early so she could organize her room and prepare for the upcoming year. It was a relief to be among her friends and away from her dependent mother.

She looked over her assigned rotations. She would have obstetrics and psychiatric nursing. That would mean six months away from the adult medical-surgical floors. This was going to be a tolerable year. She would have to endure three months of med-surg before OB.

Finally they were on the maternity floor. She had labor and delivery for the first part of the rotation. Postpartum and nursery would follow. Within an hour of reporting for duty, she was assigned to observe in the delivery room and help where needed. Marcia was deeply moved by the experience. She was awed to be present at the moment this tiny human being emerged from the womb and unfolded like a flower opening its petals to the sun. Could anything be more amazing? She was ecstatic. Miss Cline had to come and remind her that she needed to leave for lunch and afternoon classes. She rushed upstairs to find Judy. She could hardly wait to share her experience.

"You really like OB?"

"Who wouldn't? You mean to tell me you didn't like the rotation?"

"It was okay. I didn't like the smells or all the blood. I think med-surg is more challenging. I feel like a nurse can really make a difference there."

"Well, I've found my niche. I'm gong to work in Labor and Delivery. I think a good labor nurse can make a tremendous difference for those mothers."

"I think it's boring. You wouldn't want to waste your training on that would you? You're a good med-surg nurse. I've seen you with the patients."

"Say what you want. I love OB. I'm going to work there. You love caring for the sick. It just depresses me. You don't like OB. Let me enjoy it."

Marcia was inspired and humbled by the strength of these mothers who worked to bring new life into the world. They were separated from their loved ones and labored in two- or four-bed rooms with other women and then, when they were in such pain, they were hauled to the sterile confines of the delivery room. She sat by the sides of her patients and sponged their brows, adjusted their pillows, rubbed their hands and often swollen feet, and whispered any comforting words she thought might help. She coached their efforts to push, and received each newborn from the obstetrician as if it was her own child. She considered herself privileged and blessed to share in so intimate a moment of these women's lives.

Nursing now had a burning purpose for her. She would do whatever she had to so as to work with the laboring mother.

Each student was assigned a case study. Marcia was only two weeks into the rotation when her selected patient delivered early one evening. As she sat at the L&D counter finishing her notes, she heard screams from the farthest room in the labor corridor.

Marcia looked at the charge nurse.

"Who's that?"

"Just that unwed prime-ip in labor room 10. She's scared to death."

"Is anyone with her?"

"We can't spare a nurse right now. Maybe some Demerol will quiet her down."

"Can I please stay and help her?" she asked her instructor.

"It's going to be a long night. She's in really early labor and not moving any too quickly."

"It's okay. I'd like to help her."

"I'll excuse you from class tomorrow, but you will need to do a care plan and summary of the labor and delivery."

Marcia was elated.

The charge nurse looked at her.

"We put her at the end so she wouldn't disturb the others, but you know how the screaming carries."

"Could we hold the meds for a bit?"

The charge nurse nodded.

"She's the resident's patient. Dr. O'Connor is covering tonight. He's in the sleep room if you need him."

Marcia headed to labor room 10.

The young woman in the bed was near Marcia's age. Her blonde hair was disheveled. Her lips were dry, her face flushed and covered with traces of dried tears. She had a terrified expression on her face. She was starting a contraction when Marcia entered. She gripped the side rails and thrashed back and forth. The forming scream started as a moan and then became a shriek of fear and dissolved back into a helpless moan.

"Margaret, I'm here to help you."

"No one can help me." Margaret's voice was utterly desolate.

"I'll stay with you. I won't leave. Let me get you a fresh pillow case and change the pad under you. Then I'll sponge you off. You've been working hard."

Marcia proceeded to do what she proposed. When the next contraction started, she took Margaret's hand.

"Look at me, Margaret. Breathe with me. No, try not to tense up. Just breathe with me."

The scared eyes met the confident, peaceful ones and Margaret began to relax.

So they worked together for the next hour. Between contractions, Marcia finished her tasks and began brushing Margaret's tangled hair.

"Your touch makes me feel better, especially when you rub my back and shoulders."

"I'm glad."

"I didn't mean to get pregnant. John told me that he loved me and would marry me if anything happened. When I told him about the baby, he left."

"What did your parents say?"

"I didn't want to embarrass them. I haven't told them. They would be so upset. I told them I was busy with work and school, but would try to come home for the holidays. I'm adopting out, you know. I hope the agency finds a good home for my child. I love him so much already."

"So you think you're having a boy?"

"No, I just call the baby 'him'. Better than saying it."

Two hours passed in shared confidences and encouragement. Margaret calmly and with purpose gave herself over to labor, while Marcia spent herself physically doing whatever comforted her charge.

"I think my contractions are getting harder."

Marcia's hand was resting on Margaret's abdomen.

"They are stronger and longer. I've been timing them. That's a good sign. You also have more show. Notice anything else?"

"I'm a bit nauseated and my lower back hurts during the contractions."

"I'll get Dr. O'Connor after your next contraction."

"You're going to leave me?" Margaret sounded panicky.

"Just long enough to get the doctor. I promise I'll hurry."

The physicians' sleep room was dark. *Why don't they sleep facing the door, for heaven's sake, and why don't they sleep on the bottom bunks if they're empty ?* Marcia was teetering on the frame of a lower bunk and trying to peer over the shoulder of a slumbering physician in the top bunk. Suddenly, she realized that she had no idea what Dr. O'Conner looked like. She climbed down from the bunk, took a deep sigh, and called loudly.

"Dr. O'Connor!"

A form in the next set of bunks moved. A few other physicians muttered something about disturbing their sleep.

"Dr. O'Connor?" Marcia whispered loudly.

"I'm coming."

Marcia waited outside the sleep room. A tall, muscular man with tousled black hair emerged. As he put on his glasses, he asked,

"What do you need?"

"I'd like you to check your patient. I think she's making progress."

"Which one? I have two in labor."

"The primeip in labor room 10."

"Mrs. Johnson told me she would take all night plus some. Are you sure she needs to be checked?"

"Please come."

"Alright, I'll be right there."

Marcia returned to the labor room. Margaret was in the middle of a contraction. She was griping the side rails and breathing frantically.

"It's okay Margaret, I'm here."

"What took you so long?" Margaret gasped as the contraction waned.

"I just had to find your doctor."

Marcia was rubbing Margaret's shoulders when Dr. O'Connor entered. She had the glove and gel waiting for the physician. Marcia coached Margaret with great tenderness unaware that Dr. O'Connor was watching her intently.

He gently checked Margaret. "She's seven centimeters," he said with disbelief.

"You won't be much longer. You've made really good progress. Do you still want to be put to sleep when the baby is delivered?"

"No. If Marcia stays with me, I think I can do this myself."

Dr. O'Connor studied Marcia for a moment.

"Okay. We'll plan on a local for the episiotomy. Has anyone explained delivery to you?"

"Oh yes, Marcia covered labor and delivery with me."

Dr. O'Connor paused at the door observing patient and nurse for several minutes.

"I'll be at the nurses' station when you need me. Would you like me to tell the charge nurse that we need a delivery room opened ?"

"Oh please. I've completely forgotten to alert the charge nurse."

"Probably because of your total involvement in coaching." He smiled at her as he closed the door.

Dr. O'Connor was a third year resident and would be doing the delivery by himself. Marcia saw his proctor dozing at the nurses' station as she pushed Margaret's bed to the delivery room. Mrs. Elwood, one of the regular staff, was going to assist Dr. O'Connor as Marcia would be working with Margaret.

In very little time Margaret delivered.

"It's a girl!" Dr. O'Connor called out.

"Oh let me see her!"

Dr. O'Connor held the squalling newborn in the air for Margaret to view.

Mrs. Elwood hurried over to him and whispered,

"She's adopting the baby out. Just give her to me and I'll put her in the warmer."

"When can I hold her?" Margaret searched the room longingly.

"We'll just get her warmed up a bit," replied Mrs. Elwood.

"But I want to hold her."

Mrs. Elwood ignored Margaret and became absorbed in helping the doctor. Marcia stroked Margaret's forehead.

"Just be patient," she whispered.

When the post delivery exam was finished and Mrs. Elwood left the room to get warm blankets for Margaret's transfer to recovery. Marcia saw her chance. She jumped off the stool by the head of the delivery table and hurried to the warmer. In a second she was back at Margaret's side.

"Here's your beautiful girl."

Margaret was like all new mothers. She caressed the soft cheeks with her finger tips and then with her lips. She was marveling over the tiny fingers when Mrs. Elwood reentered the room. She pulled Marcia aside.

"Why did you give her that baby?"

"Because 'that' baby is her child and she wants to see her."

"We don't let adoptive mothers see their children."

"If she adopts, this is the only time she'll have to get to know her daughter."

"You haven't done her any favors. It will just make it harder to part with the child. Take the baby to the nursery as soon as possible."

"I'm accompanying her to recovery. I'll take the baby from her there." Marcia kept the rest of the sentence to herself, *after she's had plenty of time with her baby.*

"I think you're making a big mistake. I don't know what they're teaching students these days. I'll be speaking to your instructor about this."

"I understand." *Even if they kick me out, I would do the same thing again*, Marcia thought to herself.

Dr. O'Connor visited Margaret in the recovery room. His visit couldn't have been better timed. Marcia was in a corner of the room being scolded by another nurse about her inability to follow the usual protocol.

"Dr. O'Connor, would you tell Miss Burton that Margaret is your patient and you don't mind her visiting with her baby in the recovery room?" Marcia implored quietly.

Liam O'Connor was caught off guard for only a second. "It's certainly alright with me if the baby is doing well."

"You can do all the care yourself, Miss Gardinier!" With that, Miss Burton stormed from the room.

Marcia left Margaret to enjoy her baby, took her chart to the nurses' desk, and flopped into the chair. She was suddenly exhausted. Dr. O'Connor was writing orders.

"Are you alright?"

"I'm fine. It's like coming down from a great high and more practically, I just remembered that I forgot to eat dinner!"

"I'll get you some juice. I'm sure Miss What's-Her-Name won't be pleased to see you again. In any case, if we both get in trouble, you'll be pleasantly inclined to vouch for me since I've treated you so nicely."

She had not thought about any possible consequences for the resident. She looked at him in alarm. Then she noticed his slightly lopsided grin and his twinkling green eyes.

"Yeah right." She couldn't help laughing.

Marcia visited Margaret often during her three day stay and marveled at her strength and unselfish love for her child. They cried and hugged each other that last day.

"Are you going to stay in Denver?"

"No, I think I'll go back to Omaha and live near my family. I'll get a job there and finish my final year."

Later that morning Margaret left without her daughter. Marcia never heard from her again, but she never forgot her.

Despite the irate reports to her instructor from Mrs. Elwood and Miss Burton, Marcia received an A for her care of Margaret.

"Making the hospital experience more humane is exactly what I want you to do. Good job," said her instructor.

Chapter *Twenty-six*

Marcia and Liam spotted each other as soon as she entered the rec. room. She was sure he'd never been to one of their dances before and she was pleased to see him.

"I haven't had a chance to thank you for your help with my patient," Marcia said. "I haven't seen you in OB."

"I'm no longer in OB. I'm finishing up my last year rotating through surgery and the ER."

"This is your last year of residency?"

"Yep. Why don't we dance while we talk?"

He guided her onto the floor. He was not as tall as many of the men she had dated, perhaps six-one. Suddenly height did not seem so important to her.

They talked about his large family and his intention to practice in Denver. Her answers about her own family were short, but she was eager to discuss her decision to work in OB after graduation.

"You're a junior, right ?"

"Yes, and I can hardly wait to be finished."

"Why the rush?"

"Then I'll be able to do only OB. I really don't care for med-surg."

"You were very good with that old man who had his leg amputated last year."

"How do you know about that?"

"I was doing a rotation on eleven at that time."

"I don't remember you being there."

"I know. I think you were interested in that extern. Was his name Smith?"

"No, I think I remember it being Jerk or something similar. My boyfriend and I had just broken up and I was kind of looking."

"Still kind of looking?"

"I suppose. Maybe I don't know what to look for." Marcia was embarrassed to sound so wistful and she started to laugh. "I think there must be a song in there somewhere." He studied her face.

"I meant to tell you that I thought you did an amazing job with that young unwed mother."

"You mean Margaret?"

Liam nodded. He listened as Marcia described Margaret in the most complimentary fashion. She finished by stating,

"I don't know if I could be so strong."

"I suspect you're stronger than you give yourself credit for."

As they climbed the stairs at the evening's end, Liam turned to her.

"Do you like board games and things like charades?"

"I love them."

"Would you like to go out with me next Saturday? We have a group that meets once a month for a potluck and games."

"What time and what should I bring?"

"I'll pick you up at six and I'm bringing drinks, so don't worry about bringing anything else."

Marcia went to her room instead of joining the others. She wanted a few minutes to think about Liam O'Connor. He was different from the others she had dated. Something in the way he treated her. He didn't try to sneak a kiss when they were dancing, she didn't have to move his hand from her fanny as she did with so many of the other guys, and he didn't hold her so tightly that she couldn't breathe. She felt he was definitely interested in her. There was a certain feeling of rightness in being with him. Yet, something was different. She could hardly wait for Saturday.

Chapter *Twenty-seven*

Marcia was glad that Liam was fifteen minutes early. She'd been ready for the last half hour. She had looked herself over in the mirror at least three times, re-combed some imagined errant patch of hair, checked and rechecked her lipstick, and finally went to Judy's room so she could watch the front door.

Judy had laughed at her.

"You'd think this was your very first date."

"Well it is OUR first date."

"So?"

"He's just so nice. I can't believe he could possibly like me."

"Why wouldn't he like you? Why shouldn't you date a nice guy? You've certainly dated some losers lately. It's way past time for a change."

"You're right." Marcia agreed, but she had difficulty believing that that could be true.

Finally she was called to the parlor.

"You look great," Liam smiled at her.

"Thank you. So where are we headed?"

"My sister Moira's. She and her husband have an old house on LaSalle. We meet there every week. Three times a month to pray and once a month for a social evening."

"Is this a family gathering?"

"No, just a group of people trying to live our faith. My sister Fiona and her fiancee and my brother Seamus with his girlfriend will be there."

"What beautiful and unusual names."

"My dad's Irish and my mom's French, so we have Irish first names and French middle names."

"What's yours?"

"Sebastian."

"Oh. I like it."

It was a short drive to the brightly lit white two-story frame house. Liam opened her door and helped her from the car.

"Can I give you a few things to carry?"

Marcia nodded and she became the recipient of two bottles of wine.

He lifted a case of soda from the trunk. Liam waved to his sister, Fiona, and her fiancée James, who were approaching the walk from the opposite direction. He made introductions and bent to kiss his sister on the cheek.

"What's in the bag? Something good I'll bet."

"It's your favorite casserole. Just make sure to save some for everyone else."

Fiona was a very pretty woman with dark red hair and the same green eyes as her brother. When she smiled, her full lips parted to reveal perfect white teeth. Her direct gaze was open and welcoming. Marcia immediately liked her and hoped they would be friends.

After a short period of prayer, the group divided into two teams of ten for a rousing game of charades. Marcia was always competitive and became even more so after she found there were established time limits and scores kept. She and Fiona managed to propose several sayings that stumped the others. Liam, who had been on the opposing team, joined her when charades was finished.

"You guys killed us. I don't think we should put you and Fiona on the same team again."

"We could put you on our team and you wouldn't have to worry about being so soundly trounced," Marcia teased.

"Are you going to whine about being beaten?" Fiona added, "You need to be on the losing team once in a while. Besides, a little humble pie won't hurt you."

"I am humble."

Fiona rolled her eyes and replied, "Right, how could I forget?"

Liam turned to Marcia. "Would you like to get something to eat? There's quite a spread in the kitchen and you've only had a coke."

They joined the line circling a large table. Moira was fussing over the guests trying to insure they had enough on their plates. She came across the kitchen to Liam and Marcia to chat with them.

She was at the end of her pregnancy and rubbed her lower back while she talked. Moira had the same open friendliness as her siblings and was equally pretty as Fiona, but resembled neither of them. She had hazel eyes and strawberry blonde hair that was pulled into a knot at the nape of her neck.

"I'm so glad that you could come. Liam has said some very nice things about you."

"They're all true too," Marcia replied. Moira laughed. "Your house is lovely. I think old houses are the best."

"I wish we could have left the Christmas decorations up until the Feast of the Presentation, but I'll be too busy with the baby then, so they came down early."

"When are you due?"

"In two weeks, but I wouldn't mind being early."

They returned to the living room and found chairs next to the fire. Liam sat beside her with his arm draped over her chair. There was a lively discussion concerning the new birth control pill. Most felt that Pope Paul IV would not approve it.

"Even if he did, I would not want Fiona taking it. I think it does something to the marriage relationship," James stated, as he gently rubbed Fiona's hand.

"Have you seen all the side effects?" Liam asked. "Some women are

127

going to have serious health problems and die. Who would want to put their wife at such risk?"

Marcia felt that she was going to need to do some reading on the subject. Her thoughts were interrupted. Liam was asking her a question.

"What are your thoughts on the pill?"

"I can't see how putting artificial hormones in your body can be good. It's got to affect other systems in the body. I've always thought that one of the purposes of marriage was children and their guidance and care."

He nodded in agreement.

"So you'd like children?"

"I've wanted a large family for several years now. What about you?"

"I come from a large family and I see all the joys and hassles it entails. I watch my parents and wonder how they do it sometimes, then I see that bond of love and respect they have for one another and I know it's right, something desirable. Their love and faith formed all of us. I want that type of relationship for myself."

Marcia could only nod, she was so profoundly touched. They left a bit early as she had to be in by twelve-thirty.

"Did you enjoy the evening?"

"Very much. I really liked your family and friends. When are James and Fiona getting married?"

"I expect they'll marry towards the end of the year. They've known each other since high school and started dating last year. The family really likes James. He's a good man and Fiona is a great gal. They should be very happy. Before I forget, Fiona thought you might want to join us next week for prayer."

"I would like that a lot. Should I bring my Bible?"

"And your rosary."

"What about Seamus and Angelica ?"

"They met when both volunteered to work at a mission school. They didn't get a chance to date much as the work was quite consuming and they came from separate colleges. Both sets of parents cautioned them at the time. They were too young and I think everyone was concerned the race difference might be difficult in the states. They reconnected about six months ago and have been dating ever since."

The parked cars in front of the dorm were occupied with couples saying goodbye for the night, some rather passionately. Liam seemed not to notice. He came around and opened her door as soon as they were at the curb. He took her arm and walked her to the door. Another couple was kissing on the stairs.

"I had a really great time tonight," Marcia smiled up at him. "Thanks for asking me."

She was expecting a kiss. Instead, Liam opened the door and bade her goodnight.

"I'll call you about Wednesday." Then he was gone.

"Evidently he doesn't believe in kissing on the first date and it sounds like his ideas about women, marriage, and family are very traditional," Judy replied when Marcia told her about the evening.

"Well, he is very polite; opens my doors, walks on the outside of the sidewalk, helps me with my coat, and is very attentive to my comfort. He and his family are wonderful. They are definitely different."

"In what way?"

"I think they're really committed Christians."

"And that's bad?"

"No, it's good. I just don't think I measure up."

"Why don't you just relax, enjoy his company, and give yourself some credit ?"

"Okay. How much do I owe you for this session?"

After a pause Marcia asked, "How are you and Steve doing?"

"He's a great guy. Intelligent, funny sense of humor, kind, and I think he's going to ask me to marry him."

"Can I be a bridesmaid?"

"How about, do you love him and are you going to accept?"

"You've already told me you love him, so why wouldn't you accept?"

"Marriage is about more than being in love you know. Yes, I am going to accept and you can be a bridesmaid."

They squealed and hugged each other. Marcia was so happy for her friend. Usually the announcement of a pending engagement would elicit feelings of envy and of desperation that she would never find anyone.

Tonight she rejoiced with her friend. She was starting to realize that some things are worth waiting for and that marriage, the calling and covenant, was not something she could pursue and make happen; that perhaps the author of the covenant had His own plans for her. Judy had reminded her that love, albeit an extremely important reason for marriage, was not the sole basis for a successful marriage.

Chapter *Twenty-eight*

Marcia was assigned to the nursery for her final month of Obstetrics. She agreed wholeheartedly with Judy that this was the most boring part of nursing. She enjoyed helping the new mothers care for their babies, but she longed for the excitement and challenges of the delivery room. She occasionally saw Liam in the halls or elevators and was delighted when he could join her for meals in the main dining room. His relaxed manner and sharp wit made him a pleasant meal companion.

They had been dating nearly two months, always in the company of family or friends. Marcia truly enjoyed the group and was happy to find that she fit in. She was becoming increasingly attached to Liam. She saw him as a man of faith and integrity and suspected that he would be a wonderful husband. Her focus was changing. She was beginning to examine what she could bring to a marriage and what type of partner she would be.

She attended the prayer meetings regularly. If Liam was on duty, Fiona and James would offer transportation. Marcia was slowly beginning to see God as a loving and personal father intimately interested in her life.

One such evening, James said, "Fiona tells me you two are going shopping tomorrow and I just want to thank you for getting me off the hook."

"What are you talking about?" Marcia was puzzled.

"James hates shopping. You'd think I'd asked him to cut off a hand. He whines the whole time we're in the store."

"I don't whine. I just don't understand why you have to look at the same thing in a half dozen stores before returning to the original one to get what you want."

"I told you, it's part of being a good shopper."

"Well, I just want to get in and get out."

"And that my dear, is why I'm going with Marcia. Besides you'd probably be really unhappy scouting all the baby departments, until we're looking for our own child."

"Can you pick out something for me to give Moira and Jack too?" asked James.

"Yes, but it's going to cost you." They all laughed.

Marcia and Fiona found some pink lacy outfits for little Mary Kathleen and paid a short visit to Moira. As they were leaving, Fiona asked Marcia what she was wearing to the St. Patrick's party at her parent's house.

"I haven't heard about it."

"You mean to say Liam hasn't asked you yet? What's he waiting for? It's this coming weekend."

"Maybe he's on duty."

"No, he's not. I heard him tell Mom he was bringing a date."

"Perhaps he's bringing someone else." Marcia tried to sound casual even with the hard knot in her stomach.

"Marcia, he's not bringing anyone else. He's been interested in you for over a year."

"What are you talking about?"

"I probably shouldn't have said anything, but my brother's noticed you for over a year. Promise me you won't tell him I mentioned it."

"I promise you I won't say a word, but why didn't he ask me out before now?"

"You were dating others and he'd heard..." Fiona caught herself. Her cheeks flushed. "I'm sorry. I have a big mouth."

"What did he hear?"

"I don't really know specifics, but it wasn't complimentary."

It was Marcia's turn to blush. How she wished she'd been more circumspect in her dating behavior. Who said you had to kiss a lot of frogs before finding a prince? Whoever it was, was an idiot. A prince might not want someone who kissed every frog that came along.

"Can we forget I mentioned it?"

"Absolutely."

Liam joined Marcia for dinner that evening.

"Did you and Fiona have a good day shopping?"

"Oh yes, we got the cutest clothes for Mary Kathleen. We stopped to see Moira. She is doing really well. The baby is such a good nurser and so pretty."

"Did Fiona mention the St. Patrick's Day party?"

"As a matter of fact she did. She wondered why you weren't taking me."

"Why would she think I'm not taking..." Liam noticed that Marcia was grinning mischievously.

"Okay. I should have asked you last week. I'm sorry. I have so much going on that I just forgot. Can you come?"

"You're very lucky that filthy rich, handsome movie star I met is going out of town and I'm free."

"So you'll go with me by default?"

"Something like that."

Liam started to laugh.

"I'll pick you up at five. You're going to meet the whole gang, except Donal."

"Why isn't he coming?"

"He joined the Dominicans last fall."

"To be a priest?"

"Yep."

"What a blessing for your family."

Chapter *Twenty-nine*

Marcia had taken a very long time to dress and do her hair. She so wanted Liam's parents' approval. Her stomach was in turmoil and she noticed that her palms and feet were sweating; something that happened only when she was unusually nervous. She had baked an applesauce spice cake in the kitchen off the rec. room and hoped it was all the cookbook said it would be.

Liam didn't have to wait. Marcia was in the parlor almost before Mrs. Jones had the phone in the cradle.

"You look great and that cake looks even better," Liam teased as he lifted the wax paper. "What are we going to be enjoying?"

"It's an applesauce spice cake with brown sugar icing. The cookbook gave it a good review."

The O'Connors lived in what was once a farm house. The three-story clapboard and brick structure was ablaze with lights and the familiar smell of burning wood floated from several chimneys. The parents had sold the fields farthest from the house, but had saved those nearer in hopes that some of their children might want to build close by.

As they entered through the massive front door, Marcia tripped over the mat and lost control of the cake which flew from her hands. Liam was quick to grab her arm and his father, equally fast, caught the pan in mid air.

"Are you alright, my dear?" Michael O'Connor asked solicitously.

"I'm fine, just a bit clumsy," an embarrassed Marcia answered quietly.

"Well, except for the holes my fingers made in the corner, I think your cake escaped without too much damage."

Doctor O'Connor returned the cake to Marcia.

He licked his fingers, "Mmm, that's really good. I'd hug you, but I'd better go wash my hands. We're delighted to have you here."

"Well, that was an impressive entrance. I'm guessing that you're a bit nervous."

"I really am."

"Don't be. They're all going to love you," Liam rubbed her shoulder reassuringly.

They carried the cake to the kitchen and placed it on the counter. Francine, Liam's mother, held his face in her hands and soundly kissed him on the forehead. Then she turned to Marcia and grasped both her hands.

"Welcome to our home. I am so glad to meet you. You must sit next to me at dinner so we can get to know each other better." Marcia noticed that Fiona had her mother's smile.

"Do you need some help?" Marcia asked.

"No, no. You are new here. Go meet the others. Caitlin is helping me. She nodded towards a teenage girl who was chopping nuts at the opposite counter. She smiled and waved her hand. Marcia thought she could be Moira's twin.

"Happy St. Patrick's to you."

"The same to you. Oh, please cut the corner out of the cake before serving it. I had a bit of a mishap when I came in and luckily your dad rescued it."

"If those holes are from his fingers, I suspect he'll come 'round to finish the whole corner," said Francine as she surveyed the cake.

"Let's go find the others." Liam took her hand and started down the hall toward the sounds of talking and laughter.

Before they reached the closest door a tall dark-haired boy came hurtling through. He was looking over his shoulder and hit them head on. Liam pulled Marcia close and steadied her.

"Hey buddy, you'd better take the running outside."

"Oh man, I'm really sorry. I was looking for Killian." Then he noticed Marcia.

"I'm really sorry Miss. I hope you're okay."

"I'm fine. My name is Marcia."

"I'm Colm. Nice to meet you."

They shook hands, but Marcia could see that Colm was preoccupied.

"What are you two up to this time?" Liam asked.

"Nothing much, really."

"Really?"

"Well, we were sitting on the couch and Killian was trying to impress James with his knowledge of rugby. I thought, since he was so occupied, it would be a good time to tie his shoestrings together. Would you believe, he didn't even notice? Then I flicked him on the head and took off. You should have seen him when he tried to come after me. He looked like a giant bird flapping its' wings as he went down and he sounded like a distressed pig," Colm started to snort.

"Hey wise guy!"

They were joined by another tall boy. He had his mother's blonde hair and amazing gray eyes.

"Marcia, this is my brother Killian."

"Happy St. Paddy's. We're glad you could come. So Liam, how did you get such a pretty girl to accompany you?"

"Are you asking for pointers?"

Killian colored slightly. "I can do fine on my own, thank you."

Before anyone could move, he leaped through the door, grabbed Colm around the neck, and began to vigorously rub his head with his knuckles.

"Sorry about that. We had some unfinished business." He grinned and released the squirming, squealing Colm.

"So who sounds like a pig?"

Liam shook his head in amusement and guided Marcia into the room. They joined Fiona and James. Moira was nursing Mary Kathleen in a large arm chair by a roaring fire. Jack was sitting beside her. They were talking to Seamus and Angelica.

"Have you met all of the rowdies?" Fiona asked.

"I think I've met most of them."

"Did I hear that Seamus and Angelica got engaged ?" Liam queried his sister.

"You heard right." answered Fiona.

"What do the folks think ?"

"They've welcomed her into the family. Both sets of parents still have reservations on how they'll be accepted. I don't know why her parents were hesitant. After all, her father is Portuguese."

"I'm sure her parents are considering their own experiences."

"We're having a big dinner when her parents come. They'll be staying here for a few days at the end of the month.

"When are they to be married?" asked Marcia.

"In four months at St. James."

"How do you know all this?" Liam was impressed.

"She's really nosy and has great hearing," James stated and then ducked as Fiona feigned to slap the top of his head.

"Actually we arrived right behind them. I heard about the wedding when we were hanging our coats in the hall closet. And I wasn't eavesdropping. They were talking in normal tones so anyone could have heard. Seamus told me a lot of it when he dropped by my school yesterday afternoon before they went to meet mom and dad.

Francine called everyone to dinner. The whole family gathered around an enormous table. The senior Dr. O'Connor sat at the head and his wife at the foot, which was closest to the kitchen door. Angelica and Seamus sat on her left, while Marcia and Liam were motioned to her right.

As Fiona passed, she whispered in Marcia's ear, "You girls are on the grilling seats."

Angelica looked relaxed and radiant sitting next to Seamus. Marcia wished with all her heart that she had already been accepted by Francine. Dr. O'Connor said a beautiful prayer before grace, asking God's blessing for all those who had joined the family this day. Then there was a flurry of dishes passed and wine poured and they began to eat.

Since Francine already knew Angelica, she directed most of her questions to Marcia. School was the first topic and Marcia answered her questions easily. As she began to feel more relaxed, her sense of humor returned and she had the table laughing with some self-deprecating stories of her mishaps in training.

Angelica recounted how she had reconnected with Seamus when she was chaperoning a group of teen girls doing a project at the homeless shelter.

"I didn't know SOMEONE would be bringing a group of guys from another high school. It was a real job keeping the kids focused on the project. However, they settled down and worked well together, so when they wanted to go for a burger afterwards, neither of us could think of a reason not to."

"She did a great job with the girls. I asked if she'd be willing to coordinate some other activities with the guys and she said she'd consider it. We exchanged numbers."

"So how long before you called her?" asked Killian.

"I had barely gotten home and taken off my coat," Angelica smiled.

"I knew I had a rare find and decided I'd better move fast."

"He asked you out just like that? And you accepted?"

"No, I told him I'd have to think about it."

Killian persisted, "So when did you say yes?"

"When he called me back fifteen minutes later and asked if I'd had enough time to think about it."

Everyone burst out laughing.

"He was just too sincere and too charming to refuse."

"Just like his older brother," Liam added.

This comment was followed by moans and more laughter, especially after Fiona intoned, "I stand before you Lord with a humble heart."

After a lengthy meal, Francine asked for volunteers to help clear the table and serve the dessert. Marcia, Angelica, and Fiona rose at once. The men also rose, but they were clearing the table. Within minutes they were in the kitchen scraping plates and piling them by the sink.

Marcia's cake was cut into pieces and placed on a platter with another cake. Angelica's chocolate bar cookies were placed on a pretty flowered plate. Three pies were cut and all the desserts were carried to the table.

"So tell me about your family," Francine smiled at Marcia as she poured her a cup of tea.

"I was born and raised in Casper. I have two younger sisters who still live there."

"So they're both at home?"

"My youngest sister, Collette, lives with my mother. LeeAnn, who is about eighteen months younger than I, lives with her husband and two boys."

"Your father is deceased then?"

"No, my parents are divorced. My father is still in Casper too."

"Oh, I'm very sorry. The divorce must have been quite painful for you girls."

"The last time, it was more of a relief for me. My parents fought a lot."

"The last time ?"

Marcia hesitated and drew in a deep breath. She decided to tell Francine the truth, but only as much as necessary.

"I was about five the first time they divorced and around eleven the second time."

Francine could not conceal the shock in her voice.

"Your parents were married and divorced two times? So you lived with your mother?"

"Sometimes."

"Sometimes?"

"My sisters and I lived in two orphanages."

They were talking quietly, but the tone in his mother's voice had caused Liam to lean closer. He was listening intently. Marcia's heart sunk. She had never told him everything about her family and didn't want this to be the setting or the time where he learned.

Francine looked visibly shocked. She was formulating another question when Mary Kathleen, who had been sleeping in a bassinet behind her mother, began to whimper. Everyone's attention focused on the baby.

"You didn't tell me any of this." Liam's eyes searched her face.

"I didn't think it was necessary at the time. We were just getting to know each other. I haven't lied to you. I just didn't want to talk about it until you knew me better. Can we discuss this later? I'll tell you whatever you want to know," Marcia whispered.

He nodded.

The conversations had turned to lighter topics, but Marcia had difficulty joining the others. The good impression she had wanted to make on Francine seemed to be in jeopardy and she was sick at the thought that Liam might have changed in his regard for her. His arm no longer rested on her chair. Instead, he leaned his arms on the table and rested his chin in his hands as he talked.

Marcia couldn't trust herself not to cry. She excused herself and retreated to the bathroom. After washing her hands, she carefully put a bit of cold water under her eyes and blotted them on the towel. She took several deep breaths before opening the door. Fiona was waiting.

"Are you okay? What was going on at that end of the table?"

"If I tell you now, I'll cry. We can talk tomorrow if you have free time."

"Marcia, I'll always have time for you. I've only known you a few months and I already think we'll be friends forever. I'll call you tomorrow.

She hugged Marcia firmly.

"It's my turn for the bathroom. I tell you, between the tea and the wine..." She closed the door.

Marcia slowly returned to the dining room. It was empty except for Colm and Killian who were clearing the table.

"The guys are cleaning up. Your tea is on the buffet. You can join the ladies in the family room," Killian nodded toward the door.

"Thank you."

Marcia smiled, took her cup and saucer, and went down the hall. She was able to find a seat near Moira and joined the others in cooing at the baby.

She had barely finished her tea when Liam entered the room with their coats and her purse in his arms.

"We're wrapping it up in the kitchen, Mom. I've got to head out. I have a paper to present tomorrow."

"I'm sorry you have to leave so early, dear." She and Dr. O'Connor accompanied them to the door.

"It was so nice to meet you," they chorused.

"We'll have to have you for dinner soon," said Dr. O'Connor.

Marcia nodded, "I'd like that."

As they watched them go down the walk, Michael put his arm around Francine. "I like her. She seems like a good match for Liam."

"I'm not so sure. Her family history is really bad and I'm sure there's a lot she doesn't talk about."

"Really?" He raised his eyebrows. "You have to fill me in, but I do like her. And Liam seems happier than he's been in a long time."

Chapter *Thirty*

"There's a coffee shop on the way back. Since you don't have to be in 'till twelve-thirty, we'll have a bit over two hours to ourselves. Does that sound okay?" Liam's voice was restrained.

"That's fine with me, but won't it take time from your paper?"

"I said I had to present one tomorrow. I didn't say it wasn't finished."

They settled in a back booth and ordered tea. As soon as the waitress had set the pots on the table and returned to talk with a customer at the counter, Marcia began.

"I don't want you to think that I would lie to you. There are some things a person doesn't share with others, at least not right away."

"I guess I can understand that, but I was hoping you had some faith in me,"

"It's not that. As I said, I just wanted us to know each other better. Anyway...

At first, she only glanced at his face, but as she continued talking she noticed a gentleness about his features and when she met his eyes, she was comforted.

"So that's pretty much it."

"And you still talk with both of your parents?"

"Some. My father is hostile to the church and hasn't been very involved in our lives since his marriage, but we're somewhat alike in the way we think, so I feel closer to him than my mom. She is so different, she drives me nuts. But they're my parents and I owe them. I try to be as respectful as I can."

"I'm surprised you're not shy of marriage and family life."

"No, I long to have my own home and family. Any other questions?"

"Not right now."

"Do we have any time for me to grill you about your childhood?"

Liam laughed.

"You've met everyone but Donal and tons of relatives. Let's see, what would you like to hear. I have a billion stories."

Liam regaled Marcia with childhood misadventures and soon they were laughing heartily.

"Liam, look at the clock! I'm going to be late."

He hurriedly paid for their drinks and they rushed to his car. They caught every red light. When they reached the dorm, Marcia was fifteen minutes late. They dashed up the stairs.

"I truly enjoyed meeting your family. Thank you for asking me." Marcia hurried through the door and went to sign in. Mrs. Mac was waiting for her.

"You do know you're late Miss Gardinier?"

"Yes, I'm very sorry."

"I'll leave a note for Sister. She will see you in the morning."

Marcia signed in and decided to take the stairs instead of the elevator to her room on the third floor. She felt like she could fly, her spirits were so high. Liam still cared for her. Nothing else mattered.

Sister sent for Marcia right after morning Mass. She was not unsympathetic to Marcia's story, and since this was her first infraction, Marcia was given the loss of privileges for one evening. Marcia chose the coming Friday.

"You got off lightly. What did you do, cry?" Judy teased her. They were sitting on the beds in Marcia's room.

"No, it's my first infraction. So how many have you gotten?"

"A big zero if you must know."

"Guess we'll have to canonize you," said Marcia laughing.

"So, how did last night go?"

They had just started talking when Marcia was notified of a phone call.

"It's Fiona. She wants to meet for coffee. Please join us."

"Are you sure?"

"I'm positive. You two get along so well. We'll have a good time."

A good time they did have, especially after Marcia explained that the difficulties of the previous night had vanished.

As Fiona dropped them off at the dorm, she said, "Marcia you know you have my support."

"And you know that I appreciate it."

Marcia would not have been so carefree had she known what Fiona was thinking as she drove away. *I should have told her that mom and dad asked Liam to come to dinner this evening. I should have warned her that she will be the topic of conversation. I'd best wait and talk to Liam. I'm not going to upset her now. Nothing may come of this.*

Chapter *Thirty-one*

L iam knew this was not just an invitation to dinner. His parents had something on their minds. He was sure it concerned Marcia. Dad seemed to like her, so did mom have reservations about her? He was certain they could be easily overcome.

His three youngest siblings were at youth group, so he and his parents had dinner in the nook off the kitchen.

"It's just soup and sandwiches."

"You put yourself out yesterday. This looks great and it certainly beats that stuff we get in the cafeteria."

His spoon was barely in his mouth when Francine asked, "How much do you know about Marcia?"

"I've observed her for over a year and I know she's bright, funny, warm, beautiful, compassionate, and upbeat. She fits right in at prayer group, and shares some solid spiritual insights. Her home life was chaotic and miserable at times, and yet she sees her life as basically good. I find that amazing."

"You know that I love you dearly and my concern is for your future. I want you and all my children to be happy...and faithful to the Lord."

"And what has this got to do with Marcia?"

"I can see why you are attracted to her..."

"It's more than an attraction, Mom."

"Just hear me out. I cannot believe that her childhood didn't do some emotional and psychological damage which would make it difficult for her to be a good wife and mother."

"I think just the opposite. I don't notice anything in her to warrant that conclusion."

"That is exactly what I'm talking about. I am concerned about her ideas regarding marriage, and her parenting skills. She's been in not one, but two orphanages. What kind of parenting skills did she learn there? Who showed her healthy coping skills? Who formed her ideas about marriage? The surface looks fine, but what about the undercurrents?"

It was Michael's turn to speak. "We're not telling you to break off the relationship. But we want you to be very, very careful. Personally, I like the girl, but marriage is a life-long commitment and it is too important to enter into with the wrong person."

"Well, I'm not perfect either."

A long and sometimes intense discussion followed. Finally Liam reluctantly promised his parents that he would heed their advice and evaluate Marcia in light of their concerns.

"But in the end, if I decide Marcia is right for me, I want her to be accepted without reservation."

His parents agreed.

"Just a little time and distance, Liam. Just a little time."

"That won't be hard. Marcia leaves for psych in Pueblo at the end of the month. She'll be back only on the weekends. You do remember that I'll be twenty-eight in August? I'm not waiting forever. I'll give it a little time."

Liam kissed his mother and hugged his father. "Thanks for dinner."

He was out the door before they could say any more.

"I'm not so sure we should have said so much. He looks like a scolded puppy."

"I don't think it's that bad, but I'd rather he be unhappy now than later. We know the hard work marriage takes, even with a great partner." Francine's eyes followed her oldest child.

"Are you trying to tell me something?" Michael glanced at his wife.

"Absolutely. I have a great partner whom I adore and a wonderful life."

She put her arms around his neck and stretched up to kiss him. They were still in each other's embrace when Killian called from the back door.

"We're home. Youth group ended early. Can we get some hot chocolate?

Chapter *Thirty-two*

Liam parked his car and walked to the hospital chapel. He half sat, half knelt in the dimness and rested his head on his folded arms. He had waited to date Marcia for over a year, and now his parents were cautioning that he wait some more. What right had they to say anything?

It was then he remembered how they had influenced Moira to give up Paul Smith. They had seemed crazy about each other and yet his parents had flat out told her she would be miserable if she married him. Moira had protested vehemently and cried more than Liam thought it possible for anyone to cry. In the end, she did give it more time. She went to Europe for three months with her cousin. Paul's letters dropped off after eight weeks. Moira thought this was in anticipation of her return. Paul was not anticipating anything of the sort. He couldn't be alone for even two months. He was already seeing someone else. She was crushed.

She met Jack a year later. To look at her life now, he couldn't imagine her with anyone else. They didn't have the outwardly exciting relationship she had had with Paul, but there was a quiet, ardent love that permeated their marriage. Moira seemed truly happy and content.

He couldn't pray. The words wouldn't come. Finally he pushed himself onto the pew and sat with his arms across his chest for a very long time.

The anger roiling in his heart was subsiding and he began to consider his parents' words.

What could he say to Marcia? He had just assured her that her family life wasn't an obstacle for him. He was loath to hurt her and he knew she would be hurt. She was leaving in less than two weeks. He wouldn't say anything right now. He had a heavy call schedule this coming week. She could attend the Wednesday night prayer group with James and Fiona. Friday, she had a detention and he was not free on Saturday. That would leave him only one week before she was gone. He could think more clearly if he didn't see her everyday.

He did see her in the cafeteria line the next day. Her eyes had a questioning look.

"How was dinner with your parents?"

"It was fine."

"I hoped you'd call when you got back."

"It was too late. Can we meet after dinner?"

She nodded.

It was a miserable day for Liam; and for Marcia, it was a day dogged by a nagging sense of foreboding. She was relieved when Liam stopped her in the hall and suggested they go out for dinner. She had not wanted to discuss anything personal in the parlor, in the cafeteria, or at the residents' quarters.

They went to the familiar cafe by school. She wanted nothing but tea and chocolate cake which she picked apart while Liam tried to eat a hamburger.

"So what's going on?"

"My parents have some reservations about our relationship."

"What kind of reservations?"

"They think it's too soon for us to be serious and have a few other concerns."

"What other concerns?" Marcia persisted.

"Mom worries that your home life or lack of it may have had some negative effects on your ability to be a good wife and mother."

149

He had not meant to answer with such candor, yet it was necessary she know the truth. It took no amount of astuteness to see the pain in her face.

Marcia was stunned. She struggled to keep the tears from welling up in her eyes. Her voice was barely audible when she spoke. "And are you now of the same opinion?"

"No, but I told my parents I'd consider what they said and give us some more time."

"Do you think I'm unable to learn if something is lacking?"

"I have never entertained that thought. Ever ! My parents are just concerned for our happiness." His voice was tense.

Marcia quickly slid from her seat and pulled on her coat. "I really need to get back to the dorm."

She walked to the door and waited while he paid the cashier. Liam broke the silence as they drove toward the hospital.

"In all fairness, you must admit that my parents are right; we haven't known each other that long. They've been good advisors to all of us and I feel I owe their concerns some consideration."

"So what do you want to do?" Marcia's voice was strained.

"You'll be leaving for Pueblo in less than two weeks and I've volunteered to work in a clinic in Appalachia."

"When did this come about?"

"The need was just posted on the board and I took it. I leave the week after you do and I'll be gone for six weeks. My schedule is crammed this week due to the change, but I'd like us to go to dinner the Saturday before you leave. I'll have my post office box by then. Would you consider writing to me?"

"Yes, of course I'll write."

"I'll call you about Saturday."

There seemed to be no more to say. He walked her to the door and she entered in silence.

Her roommate was away on rotation, so the room was dark and quiet. Marcia did not turn on any lights. She curled up on her bed and let the tears fall silently on her pillow. The darkness of the room seemed brighter to her than the darkness she felt in her soul.

She was awakened by the sound of Judy tapping on her door.

"Marcia, are you alright?"

"No."

"It can't be about Liam. You said everything was fine. Bad news from home?"

"It's his mother. She doesn't think I have the qualities needed to be a good wife and mother." Marcia began to cry again.

"You're kidding! Just give her some time. She needs to know you better."

Well Liam has consented to his parents' desire to give our relationship a breather. They think we need more time. I can understand what they are saying, but I don't feel that way. What if he's reconsidering our whole relationship?"

"Asking for more time isn't the worst thing in the world. As I said, his mother just needs to know you better. I think it says something that he's willing to consider their objections."

"I know you're right.I just don't want to lose Liam, he's such a good man. I used to try so hard to be in love and turn myself inside out to please some guy. This is so very different. I'm can be myself with Liam. I've never felt this way before. I love him, Judy."

"Well, I think he truly cares for you. Patience, my friend."

"Thanks. I think I'll need more than patience. I think I'll need a ton of prayers."

"Well, I can certainly do that."

It was late and they needed to be up early the next morning for floor duty, so their conversation was short.

After Judy left, Marcia knelt by her bed. She prayed for Liam, his family, and her own. She did not pray that he would marry her. She would leave that up to God. She felt more at peace when she climbed under the covers.

Chapter *Thirty-three*

Fiona was alone when she picked up Marcia for prayer group. James was giving a talk for Catholic law students. She wasted no time telling Marcia what she thought of the whole situation and ended by saying, "I know mom is just being protective of her son's welfare, but honestly, I think she's really wrong this time."

"How did you find out about this?"

"Liam and I are close. I had called him about tonight and he sounded down. I asked him if I could help. He wanted me to pick you up and he asked me to pray that he makes good decisions. You two got on so well. He seemed so content. I'm betting everything is going to be fine. So what can I do to help?" She turned to Marcia.

"Just be my friend and pray for us. You know this is my last Wednesday for awhile. I'm going to Pueblo on Sunday."

Marcia did not want to think that it could be her last time, period.

"Oh. I'd forgotten about that. You'll be back in Denver every weekend, right? Promise you'll call me?"

"I promise."

Liam caught her in the cafeteria the next day. "How about five on Saturday?"

"That sounds fine. Are Fiona and James coming with us?"

"No, I'd like it to be just the two of us."

They decided on a small bar and grill. Marcia was surprised that the place was so empty for a Saturday night.

"I think it picks up after the movie's first showing. I know you'll like the food."

Marcia had noticed background music and she smiled as she scanned the menu. 'A Train' was playing on the jukebox.

"I like the music already. These are my kind of songs."

"They have all the great songs of the 20's through the 40's."Liam said as he looked through the selections in the wall box on the table. He dropped a quarter in the slot and pushed the buttons for five selections. When they had finished ordering, he suggested they dance.

"Now?"

"Sure. What do you think that dance floor's for?" He nodded towards a tiny wood floor which was empty.

The strains of Stardust floated over the subdued voices of the other patrons.

"Oh, I love that song."

"I know."

"Are you responsible for choosing it?"

"I am, unless someone else requested it first."

Marcia put out her hand. "Let's not waste another bar of it."

It was easy to follow Liam as they floated around the floor. When the last note had played, Marcia turned toward the booth, but Liam held her in place.

"I'll bet there's another of your favorites coming up."

They remained on the floor until their plates were on the table.

The relaxed atmosphere and the lovely romantic old tunes put them both at ease. It was as if no unpleasantness had ever existed between them. They ate and returned to the dance floor until the noisy theater crowd arrived.

It was barely eight-thirty when they stepped into the chilly air.

"I don't think our rec. room is being used tonight. We can have some tea and sit and talk for awhile," Liam suggested.

"Anything out of this wind will suit me," Marcia replied as she bent her head against a bone chilling blast from the early spring storm.

Liam has been right. The room was empty. People wandered in and out as if looking for something to do, but left after exchanging greetings with them. They sat at one of the tables, drinking their tea and playing Scrabble while they discussed their upcoming assignments and whatever else came to mind.

As they walked across the parking lot to her dorm, Marcia again promised to write.

"I like to write, so you may get a couple of letters a week, unless I get no response. Then you won't get so much as a postcard," she jokingly threatened him.

"I don't have your new address. Do you want me to send my letters to the school or wait until you know your address at psych?"

"Send them to the school. I'll pick them up when I come back on weekends."

As he opened the door for her, she spun around and kissed him lightly on the cheek. She called over her shoulder as she entered the foyer, "Hope you have a great experience."

I probably shouldn't have done that, she thought as she went to her room. *Oh well, it's too late now. What was I thinking? Time and patience, time and patience. Boy, I'm not good at this.*

Marcia had caught Liam by surprise. She had barely brushed his cheek with her lips and yet it was enough to make him feel light hearted. The icy wind didn't feel nearly as brutal as it had when they had walked to her dorm. He had appreciated her spontaneity from the beginning. This thought made him smile. It would be a long six weeks. He knew that she would be true to her promise and write often.

Chapter *Thirty-four*

The state hospital at Pueblo had an affiliation with a wide range of nursing schools which meant that Marcia and her classmates got to meet women from nursing programs in other states. Everyone compared uniforms. Some of the caps were quite unusual and were difficult to starch and keep in shape. Everyone, including the students who wore such caps, poked fun at them.

Marcia and most of her classmates decided in the first few days of the rotation that they did not want to work at the state hospital after graduation. All students had the full weekend free and Friday afternoons saw a mass exodus as soon as classes and floor duty were finished.

Marcia wrote short letters to Liam on class days and long letters on Saturdays. She knew he would not have time to do the same. It was, therefore, a joy to find two letters of several pages waiting for her when she arrived back at the dorm. It seemed quite different, more revealing, to see his thoughts on paper. He had a strong masculine style of penmanship and expression. To her, it was like seeing another aspect of his personality, which she found quite pleasing. She wondered what he thought of her letters.

Hers were welcomed with the same enthusiasm as she welcomed his. She was as spontaneous on paper as she tended to be in person. Her attention to incongruities of a situation and her zany sense of humor caused him to laugh more than once. Her letters came on softly colored feminine stationery, in a hand with large soft swirls. She seemed to write with utter openness. Liam also found this form of communication to be a highly satisfactory way to learn more about Marcia.

Marcia occasionally joined Fiona and James on the weekends for a movie or a visit with Moira and her family. She and Judy had little time together. Judy was busy planning her wedding and needed to make frequent trips to Cheyenne.

Marcia began reading books on etiquette, child rearing, and anything she could find on marriage and family.

She had also made a decision to see one of her teachers at psych. He was a psychologist with a private practice in Pueblo. If she was lacking in the emotional and psychological skills necessary for a successful marriage, she needed to know how to remedy it. Her appointment was scheduled on Wednesday of her third week there. Judy was the only one who knew of her plan.

"I think that's smart. You'll know your weak spots and can start to work on them. I think that reading would be a help too."

"Yes, but you know how we all think we've got some disease after we read the symptoms. Besides, I want an outside evaluation by someone who's not blinded by my stellar personality."

Marcia could not keep a straight face and both of them started laughing.

She was not laughing, however, when she entered Dr. Studer's office. Maybe it was a mistake to see a professor for an emotional health evaluation.

Well, I'm already standing in the office, so I might as well get started, she reasoned.

The receptionist greeted her cheerily and handed Marcia a clipboard. It was then she realized that she'd be paying cash and hadn't checked the amount in her wallet. She completed the paperwork and returned to the desk.

"I see you're a student. The fee is five dollars."

Marcia exhaled quietly. She had more than enough to cover the visit.

Her return to her seat was interrupted by Dr. Studer calling her name.

She followed him to a pleasant office and chose a large armchair across from the desk.

"So, Miss Gardinier, how can I help you?"

Marcia studied Phillip Studer's face for a few seconds before speaking. *He didn't look that young in class or that handsome,* she thought with some surprise.

Slowly she recounted the past weeks and ended by saying, "I guess my main reason for coming is to find out if Mrs. O'Connor's doubts are well founded and what I can do to improve myself."

The hour was almost up.

"We'll delve more thoroughly into your family history next week."

As she walked across the grounds, she thought, *What was I thinking coming to a professor? Hope this doesn't influence my grades. Wonder what he'll think of me?*

Phillip Studer already considered Marcia an excellent student and he enjoyed lecturing all the more because of her thoughtful comments and questions, and her presence in his class. She was certainly more mature than most of her classmates. He had not had time to look at the office schedule that particular day, so he was surprised to see her standing there. After she left, he stood by the window watching her walk across the grounds. He was reasoning with himself. Perhaps he should refer her to a colleague?

There's no reason I have to step aside, he told himself. *I can do a good assessment. Besides I already know one side of her.*

The following week, he probed Marcia's background and Marcia was surprised to find that she was sometimes tearful. The hour passed quickly.

"I'll need to see you next week. Are Wednesdays still good for you?"

Marcia left wishing she had not started this digging up the past, but she was not going to drop the appointments. She needed to know about herself.

The following Wednesday, she was given a battery of tests. They talked for a brief period when she was finished.

"Will you know the results next week?" she asked before leaving.

"Yes, we'll discuss them then." He suggested some reading material for her.

The following week dragged. Marcia was anxious to learn what the tests had revealed, but more importantly, she wanted the time to pass. Liam would be coming back in a little over two weeks.

"You seem to be having a good day," smiled Dr. Studer.

"Oh yes! Liam will soon be back in Denver and I can hardly wait to see him."

Marcia didn't notice a shadow pass over Phillip Studer's face. He beckoned her to a chair next to his and they reviewed her tests. She was relieved to find that the results showed a basically happy, balanced individual.

"Why are you so surprised?"

"I guess I've never had a very high opinion of myself. I still find it amazing that Liam O'Connor would be interested in me."

"Why?"

And so they talked. She was still in the chair next to him and had twisted to face him.

"So you think I'll be okay?"

"You are OK. I think you have the potential to be a fine wife and mother. Having a strong support system will be beneficial. You say he has a wonderful family. If you marry him, see if you can rely on them for support. I don't think I need to see you again unless you want additional sessions."

"No, I think I'll be fine. Thank you so much."

They rose and Marcia extended her hand to him. He took her proffered hand in both of his and held it gently.

"Have a wonderful life, Marcia. If you need anything else, don't hesitate to call."

"I won't. Thank you again."

After she had left, Phillip Studer returned to the chair behind the desk and played with his pen. She had been so close. He could still smell her perfume.

Liam O'Connor wasn't the only man who had admired Marcia from a distance. Phillip Studer had noticed her the first day of class. She was very pretty and certainly bright and funny. But those attributes were only part of the appeal. She had a certain naïve vulnerability which elicited a desire in him to protect her.

He had been extremely careful in his deportment towards her in class and had turned her assignments over to an aide at the college for correction. No, he had not betrayed himself. He would not have dated a student. He would have waited until after she left Pueblo to contact her. He had vowed to do the right thing for her and he had, but it was at some cost to himself.

Marcia almost flew across the grounds. She would be fine with help and support from those around her. She could hardly contain her joy. She reviewed all that Dr. Studer had told her. Suddenly she stopped. She shook her head.

What a dummy I am! My imagination must be working overtime.

Still, when she was sitting next to him she thought she noticed something in Phillip Studer's gray eyes. And his handshake seemed a bit long. Nevertheless, his advice had been helpful and his behavior had never been inappropriate in any way. She was just being goofy. Right now, she had better things to consider. Liam would soon be back.

Chapter *Thirty-five*

L iam couldn't wait for evening; he wanted to see her for lunch. She couldn't wait for the elevator, but plummeted down the stairs. She skidded to a halt in the hall, took a deep breath, stifled the urge to run into the room and throw her arms around his neck, and walked demurely into the parlor.

"Hi there," his familiar grin made her smile. He walked across the room and hugged her. The surprise showed on her face.

"I think we need more separations."

"Why?" he was puzzled.

"Because I get a hug when you return."

Liam laughed and took her hand.

"Come on. I'm hungry and we have lots to talk about. What were you waiting to tell me?"

"Later."

It was an unseasonably warm May day and they decided to walk around the park after lunch.

"So has later come?"

"I suppose. I was concerned about what your mother said, so I decided to have an emotional health evaluation with a psychologist at Pueblo."

"Did you really think that was necessary?"

"It turned out to be a good thing. He made me feel much better about myself and he gave me some reading material and some very good advice and insights into my feelings. It's a relief to know that I have wife and mother potential."

"I already suspected that."

They walked hand in hand with matching strides, content with each other's company. Marcia thought May had never been so glorious.

"Mother wants to have a potluck at the house tonight. I told her we'd be coming. Are you okay with that?"

Inwardly Marcia marveled at how fast a menacing little cloud could pop up on a perfectly lovely horizon.

"Does she know you're bringing me?"

"Of course. Just be yourself."

"That's easy for you to say."

"Trust me. My parents do like you."

"Oh shoot. What time is it? I need to make something to bring. Will a salad work?" Marcia asked.

"I think so. We could put it together in the kitchen off your rec. room."

"Oh no we can't. Men aren't allowed anywhere but the parlor unless there's a special activity and then they can come to the basement or the auditorium."

It was already late afternoon. They hurried to the supermarket and collected the needed ingredients for the salad and found a large glass bowl at the thrift shop before heading to the residents' building.

"Doesn't anyone ever clean this place?"

"The housekeeper comes every Monday. We have some real slobs here. Why do you think I suggested your kitchen?"

"I don't think slob is an adequate explanation for this mess," said Marcia as she scrubbed the counter.

They worked side-by-side, chatting happily as they washed, chopped, and layered.

"That didn't take as long as I thought it would. It looks pretty good, don't you think?"

Liam nodded.

"I need to get ready."

"Ready? I think you look fine. Can't you go as you are?"

"Absolutely not. I'll need a half hour. We'll still be on time."

"I'll see you in thirty minutes."

"Don't come early. I want my full amount of time."

She was ready when Liam came.

"You didn't have to change, but you look great." He walked toward her.

"You smell good too."

"See what a difference a little time to get ready makes?" she smiled at him.

Liam helped her into the car and handed her the salad.

"I'd suggest you don't make such a grand entrance this time. I don't know if dad can rescue a salad."

"You are insufferable."

Chapter *Thirty-six*

The males of the family were engaged in a wild game of kickball on the north lawn when they arrived.

"The door's open," Michael called as he sprinted after Killian. Marcia could sense that Liam wanted to join them.

"I can take the salad. Why don't you join that melee?"

"Are you sure?"

She smiled and nodded. He handed her his jacket and bounded toward the others.

"Who's team am I on?"

Marcia was surprised at how fast he could run. She watched for a moment, took a big breath, and entered the lioness' den. The women were in the kitchen. Francine was the first to spot her.

"Marcia, we are so glad you could join us. Put that lovely salad over there."

She wiped her hands on her apron and hurried toward her. Marcia was astounded when she grasped her shoulder and reached up to kiss her cheek.

"Come get a cup of tea. We'll give the men a few minutes more."

"Then they'll all be really smelly and sweaty when we sit down to eat," said Fiona in mock complaint.

Fiona needn't have worried, not that she had. Dinner wasn't served until after all the ball players had time to clean up in one of the houses' numerous bathrooms.

The gathering was larger than the previous one as the younger children had a couple of friends staying overnight. Marcia noticed Caitlin's friend eyeing Killian. She noted that Killian was unusually grown up in his behavior. She smiled as she caught him stealing furtive glances at the girl.

Marcia sat between Fiona and Angelica. Liam, Seamus, and James sat across from them. Marcia found Angelica fascinating and she was awed by her. She was a teacher like her father who was from Portugal. He had met her mother while teaching English at a Catholic college in Mozambique. Angelica was finishing her masters, fluent in four languages, and widely traveled. She dressed beautifully and had flawless manners and a pleasant voice. Seamus was right about her being a real gem. He planned to work for the foreign service and, not even considering that they seemed to love each other deeply, Angelica would be an unbelievable asset as his partner.

As Marcia listened, doubt began to gnaw at her. How could Liam, or any man for that matter, not want a woman like Angelica who had so much to offer ? Marcia had little but herself to give and a goofy family to boot. How could she even compete with such women? She had seen some of the other nurses trying to get Liam's attention when he rounded on the floor. He had always been polite, but never flirtatious. Well, maybe she didn't have to compete. This wasn't a game after all. God would direct her if she would let Him. She began to feel slightly more confident.

She glanced across the table. Liam was having a lively discussion with Seamus and James and had not noticed her looking at him. Had she never appreciated how handsome he was? An errant strand of curly black hair clung to his forehead and reminded her of a little boy who had been out in the wind. His high cheek bones were slightly flushed and his smile produced a trace of dimples.

Marcia had no more time for reflection as dinner ended soon after and she was busy with clean up. Liam had joined her at the sink and they both dried dishes while Fiona washed. Francine eschewed automatic dishwashers, saying they didn't clean well, so there was always a need for kitchen help after meals. Listening to the light hearted exchange between brother and sister made Marcia smile.

The younger siblings headed to a movie with their friends and the adults gathered in the family room when everything was done. Seamus and Angelica excused themselves shortly after. They were meeting with the priest for premarital counseling.

"I forget how close that wedding is," Fiona remarked as they left.

"Our household seems to be in the state of flux. I'm not sure I can keep up with so many changes," sighed Francine.

"You'll do fine dear. You always do." Michael rubbed his wife's shoulder and kissed her cheek.

"Aren't you two approaching a big anniversary next year?" queried James.

"Oh yes. We will celebrate thirty years."

"How wonderful!" The words from Marcia's mouth were so spontaneous and sincere that Francine smiled.

With little encouragement, the couple launched into tales of their courtship and the early days of their marriage.

Liam sat beside her, and as usual, one arm was behind her, draped over the back of the sofa. Marcia, content in his closeness, was happy to sit and listen. The pleasant evening passed all too quickly.

As they drove back to the dorm, she tried to broach the subject of her earlier discomfort.

"I got to know Angelica a little better tonight. She really is an amazing woman."

"She seems to be. Seamus certainly is happy."

"I couldn't help envying her a bit."

"Because she gets to marry Seamus?"

"What?"

He was laughing at her confusion. She punched his arm.

"Alright, why do you envy her?"

"She's so refined, and so put together, and so charming, and so..."

"...composed and elegant. She's everything that Seamus wants. They are perfect for each other."

"But..."

"How about spontaneous, witty, warm, compassionate? How about someone who has had so much against her and yet is upbeat and willing to try to learn to better herself? Don't you think those are some amazing traits?"

Marcia felt un-beckoned tears start down her cheeks. The lump in her throat prevented her from replying, so she sat quietly.

They were in front of the dorm. She looked at Liam. His eyes said all she needed. She knew that she could become the woman she was created to be; the woman he saw her to be. She smiled at him.

"It's been another great evening. Thank you."

"Believe me, the pleasure is all mine."

He helped her from the car, took her hand, and walked her to the door.

"Let's go to Mass tomorrow at the hospital chapel. We can meet for lunch when I finish rounding. It will have to be the cafeteria. I took Mitchell's call for Sunday."

"I'll bring lunch. That little restaurant down the street is open on Sundays. Even their sandwiches are better than cafeteria food."

"See you tomorrow." He hugged her and then opened the door for her.

Chapter *Thirty-seven*

The psych affiliation was finally finished. The great food in the hospital cafeteria, and later, her weekends with Liam had been the bright spots of the past three months. Dr. Stroud had been as pleasant as usual and Marcia chided herself for even thinking he'd been attracted to her.

She would have a week's vacation starting the first week of July and Liam wanted to drive her home so he could meet her family. Marcia dreaded the thought of it. She could only hope her mother would not say anything too outrageous. Her father would probably fidget anytime she sat next to Liam, but he and Velma would talk like adults. Liam would only be there for the day, so she told herself to be calm. They would leave for Casper on Sunday after Mass.

Another change was also imminent. She would not be seeing Liam in the hospital setting as much since he since he was finishing his residency and was entering private practice. She could understand Francine's complaint about adjusting to the change.

It was a surprise when Liam called on Friday to tell her that he would pick her up in Pueblo. Marcia was relieved that finals finished early so she could be ready to go when he arrived.

They were approaching Colorado Springs when he asked, "Have you seen the Garden of the Gods?"

"No. We don't stop anywhere on the way to and from Pueblo."

"Want to stop and take a look around? It's very beautiful. We'll have time."

"I'm game. When are we meeting James and Fiona?"

"When we return to Denver."

They decided on the Garden Trail. It would be a nice easy walk and introduce Marcia to the park.

"Liam, this is beautiful. Have you been here before?"

"Several times. My parents brought us frequently when we were younger."

"I would like to see it all someday."

"I think we might be able to do that."

The stunning vistas of rock and sandstone against the vibrant blue sky gave Marcia an overwhelming sense of awe at the beauty of the place and she did not hesitate to share her sentiments with Liam.

"You're so easy to please."

"How can you be such a tease? This is magnificent."

"Why don't we sit on that bench and enjoy the scenery," Liam nodded to a spot a short distance ahead of them.

She settled next to him on the bench.

"There are a lot of beautiful parks in these areas that I think you'd enjoy exploring. Do you like to camp?"

"I've never done it. I think I'd like it from what I've heard. But I want a campground with a bathroom. I'm not doing that 'days without a shower' thing."

"None of that roughing it, huh?"

"Isn't sleeping on the ground in a tent roughing it enough?"

"Yeah, that's a start."

"You guys can do the roughing it stuff." They sat in silence for a moment.

"Incidentally, I have something for you. Fiona helped me with it."

He handed Marcia an accordion folded piece of parchment bound with a gold ribbon.

"Open it one line at a time."

Marcia carefully untied the ribbon and read:
Proverbs 31: 'Who shall find a valiant woman?"
Slowly she opened each layer and read.

Who shall find a valiant woman ? Her value is far beyond pearls
Her husband entrusting his heart to her, has an unfailing prize.
She brings him good, not evil all the days of her life.
She obtains wool and flax and makes cloth with skillful hands.
Like merchant ships, she secures provisions from afar.
She rises while it is still night and distributes food to her household
She picks out a field to purchase; out of her earnings she plants a vineyard
She is girt about with strength and sturdy are her arms
She enjoys the success of her dealings; at night her lamp is undimmed.
She puts her hand to the distaff, and her fingers to the spindle.
She reaches out her hands to the poor, and extends her arms to the needy.
She fears not the snow for her household; all her charges are doubly clothed.
She makes her own coverlets; fine linen and purple are her clothing.
Her husband is prominent at the city gates as he sits with the elders of
the land.
She make garments and sells them, and stocks merchants with belts
She is clothed with strength and dignity, and laughs at the days to come
She opens her mouth in wisdom, and on her tongue is kindly counsel.
She watches the conduct of her household, and eats not her food in idleness.
Her children rise up and praise her; her husband, too, extols her
Many are the women of proven worth, but you have excelled them all.
Charm is deceptive and beauty fleeting; the woman who fears the Lord
is to be praised.
Give her a reward of her labors, and let her works praise her at the city
gates.

When she finished, she put the parchment in her lap. "That man pays
a beautiful tribute to his wife."

"You forgot to open the last fold."

"I thought it was sealed to indicate that it was the end of the proverb."

"It is the end of the proverb. The other is an addition."

Marcia broke the seal and read,

"I love you, Marcia Gardinier. Will you be my Valiant Woman?"

"Oh yes! Absolutely yes!" Then Marcia began to cry.

Liam cupped her chin in his hand and brought his face close to hers. It was the sweetest, most precious, most longed-for kiss she had ever received. Some time passed as they sat next to each other, her head resting on his shoulder. Occasionally, she could feel his lips against her hair. Finally, he shifted.

"One more thing. Let's see if this fits."

He pulled a small box from his jacket pocket and knelt in front of her. Taking her left hand, he placed the ring on her finger. Bending forward, she placed both hands on his shoulders and kissed him again.

As he reclaimed his seat on the bench, she stretched out her hand and admired her ring.

"It's beautiful. I couldn't imagine anything more perfect."

A lustrous pearl surrounded by two small square cut diamonds shone in the gold setting. She was still admiring her ring when they noticed an elderly couple coming toward them. They rose to meet them.

"Ask her to be your Misses, did you Son ?"

He grasped Liam's hand and pumped it vigorously. His wife smiled at both of them.

"We saw you propose and are so happy for you. May you have many happy years." said the grandmotherly woman.

"Yep, we've been married fifty four years. Had some pretty good ones. Some bad ones too.You just have to love each other with all the ups and downs and trust in the Almighty. Congratulations to you."

"My name's Burt and this is my lovely wife, Effie."

Taking Marcia's hand in hers, Effie admired Marcia's ring. "It does my heart good to see young love."

And so they stood and chatted, the fresh new lovers and the tested and tried older ones.

Finally Liam said they needed to be getting back to Denver.

"Well we're glad to see our bench put to such happy use."

"Your bench ?" Marcia and Liam looked puzzled.

"Oh yes, Dears. Burt and I have been coming here every evening the weather permits, for the past eighteen years. The children are all grown and it's just the two of us now."

"Yep, just me and my best girl." Burt looked lovingly at his wife.

"Enjoy your bench and the evening." Liam smiled at the couple,

"Hope we see you again.

We plan on returning."

They bid each other goodbye and Burt and Effie took their places on the bench.

"What a lovely couple." Marcia said as they walked hand in hand toward the entrance.

"They sure seem to be. We'd better pick up the pace if we're going to be on time for dinner."

"I thought you said we'd meet James and Fiona whenever we got there."

"You are such a stickler for details. We're meeting everyone at the house. They want to celebrate our engagement."

"They all know? So what would have happened if I had said 'no'?"

"We'd have gone to dinner all the same. They would have had to put away the champagne."

"Marcia smiled, "I love you, Liam O'Connor."

Suddenly Marcia stopped and faced him.

"I'm not so sure about that distaff and spindle thing."

"I think we can skip that."

"I think we'd better skip the vineyard too."

"You plan on doing all the rest ?"

"Why don't we see how things go ?"

They laughed and continued on, her hand at rest in his.

# # # # # # # # #

171

CPSIA information can be obtained at www.ICGtesting.com
Printed in the USA
LVOW040237020113

313915LV00002B/7/P